ACKNOWLEDGEMENT

Many thanks to my friend John Young

JUSTICE DELAYED

Ron Walters

Published 2011 by arima publishing

www.arimapublishing.com

ISBN 978 1 84549 504 6

© Ron Walters 2011

Printed and bound in the United Kingdom

Typeset in Garamond 11/14

Swirl is an imprint of arima publishing.

arima publishing
ASK House, Northgate Avenue
Bury St Edmunds, Suffolk IP32 6BB
t: (+44) 01284 700321

www.arimapublishing.com

CHAPTER 1

Home Secretary, Nathan Garland, sat at his desk gazing out of his office window, looking at the people in the streets rushing around; he sat day dreaming about his retirement in two years time. The past eighteen months dealing with the 5th Column discovered in Liverpool and the unpleasant happenings and the death of two of his agents has affected his health. His wife and family have urged him to take early retirement but he is adamant that he should continue until his official retirement date but he had no idea what was round the corner.

Gone was that tall smartly dressed upright man with thick black curly hair. Nathan now has a permanent stoop and a receding hairline, his hair no longer black, almost white and his family finds this most upsetting, particularly the grandchildren who expected him to go fishing or doing things, their friends do with their granddad but he is always too busy.

As he was dreaming, his phone started to ring this brought him out of his reverie?

His secretary said,

"Ken Lee is on the line, he wants to speak to you urgently."

He picked up the receiver, before he could answer; his senior intelligence officer started speaking.

"I must speak to you Nathan, the subject is too sensitive to discuss over the phone may I call round?"

"Yes, can you make it within the next hour as I have a meeting, later?"

"I'll be with you in thirty five minutes."

Nathan sat puzzling, what was so important to bring Ken dashing to his office?

Nathan was confident that Ken is such a trustworthy and experienced Intelligence officer, he must have a definite reason for his request.

Ken arrived and was shown into Nathan's office.

"Hello Ken, nice to see you again, what is so urgent for this meeting?"

"I've just come from Liverpool, where the German 5th Column had been set up in the basement of an old cinema during World War11, in readiness for when the German Army invaded Britain. It has now given up its secret."

"You will remember about this unit, you visited when the valuable Paintings and the Diamonds were discovered. No doubt you will also recall the trouble we had from several Ex Nazi Officers, they were looking for something but we did not know what. We thought they were looking for the valuables, which, had been plundered from the occupied countries and hidden by a Nazi Officer in the building but he was tried for war crimes and hanged before he could tell where he had hidden the treasure.

We know two of the seekers were British, Lord Thame and Sir Henry Grainger; they were put on trial for treason and sentenced to prison quite recently. Still, you know all about those two, you were instrumental in achieving their conviction."

Ken handed Nathan a large dirty brown envelope.

"This is what they were looking for."

"Where on earth did you find this?"

"It was pinned to the wall in the canteen behind the large Nazi Flag in the basement; it was found when they took the flag down for restoration."

*

Nathan opened the envelope; he started to read, after reading a couple of lines he slumped down into his chair.

"Good God Ken.!!

How did these people hope to achieve this?"

He looked down the list of names; there were twenty names in total, all prominent and successful businessmen. The names consisted of Eight Germans, Six British and the Six French names were all men with one exception, Madam Ackers.

The French Army shot her husband during the 1914-1918 war for treachery and I understand she is still very bitter, that must be the reason for her name to be included. She lives, or did live in a large secluded Chateau in the north of France and it is possible that is where they intended to operate from."

"What are you talking about Nathan?"

"It was common knowledge during World War11 that a group of prominent business industrialists were planning to take over the three occupied European countries, France, England and Germany and join them up as one country when the German Armies were in complete control. The people listed were going to form one government, with Germany in full control and with SS Officer Klaus Gunter at the helm. Klaus was reported as saying.

We will make the rules, France will please herself but Britain will do as she is told. If not, we will cripple Britain economically and bring Britain to her knees and would become the Beggars of the world. Each of the listed people, who were hoping to form the government, had a selected team that had been trained in readiness for the coup.

Had this transpired there would have been no Nuremberg War Crime Trials, Two of the German names on the list are now serving a lifetime prison sentence for rape and murder. Two of the British men named, were convicted and imprisoned for treason.

I will have to consult my superiors and arrange to meet my opposite numbers in France and Germany.

The wheels were put in motion and there was a lot of opposition from various quarters, however, after discussions a meeting was planned to take place. The most senior civil service officers and loyal members of the various countries involved would then discuss this new situation."

*

Several weeks later, Nathan telephoned Ken summoning him to his office. When he arrived, Nathan proceeded to relate what had taken place at the meeting, which was held in an old castle on the outskirts of Paris, to which Peter Horn MP and he attended.

"There were six in attendance, two from each country involved. They were all very senior and loyal intelligence officers and there was a seventh man in the chair who was a senior member of the German Government.

We were all very surprised when the chairman stood up and proceeded to read from a sheet of paper, which, he said were the minutes that had been taken at a meeting in Dusseldorf just prior to the invasion of Poland in 1939. The persons, who were present at this meeting, are the same names as shown on the copy of the list recently found in Liverpool. Prior to this meeting, a thorough investigation has been carried out and we have found only fourteen of the listed people are still living. There are four serving prison sentences, so that leaves ten for us to be concerned with."

One prominent French Government official stood up and made a proposition.

"The ten who are living and still free should be traced and eliminated in such a way, that no suspicion should fall on any one person.

A plausible accident should be arranged."

"Why do you say that sir?"

"I can associate several of the names you have just read out as being well known villains, they were responsible for a lot of innocent people being tortured and murdered during the war for their own benefit."

The Chairman, Count Jan Krupp turned to the meeting saying.

"Gentlemen, go away and consider this serious proposal very carefully and return here one week today. On your return we will take a vote."

"Before I go on Ken, shall we have a cup of coffee?"

"I returned to Paris last Tuesday and stayed for a couple of days and the meeting was certainly an eye opener."

The Count opened the meeting.

"Before you take a vote on the serious proposal placed on the table at our last meeting, I must tell you that I have a complete dossier on each of the names in question and each one has become very prosperous business people."

"Now to business, on the table in front of you is a voting paper, you can vote on the proposal that the remaining ten should be eliminated, put a cross for or against.

When you have decided, fold your paper and place it in the box at the end of the table."

The six men cast their votes and placed the papers in the box.

"Right gentlemen, I'll tip the papers from the box on to the table and you can watch as the votes are counted."

The six men sat and watched and to their surprise, the proposal was carried unanimously, the six people present had voted to eliminate the remaining ten who were regarded as being treacherous to benefit their own ends.

"I have put ten pieces of paper in this small black bag and on each slip of paper is the name of the traitors to be eliminated."

Pointing to the man sat next to him.

"Kindly take one name from the bag."

He put his hand into the bag and pulled out a piece of paper, which he handed to the chairman.

"The first name to come out of the bag is Pierre Ingle."

The chairman opened his brief case, holding up a folder.

*

"The dossier on this man is.

He was employed in one of the government offices in Paris and when the German army attacked France and when they capitulated he took on the job as planned in Dusseldorf.

He became a very vicious man and he passed on information to help the SS Troops round up the members of the various resistance groups. He personally shot several young boys and their fathers just to convince the Germans he was loyal to their cause. It was reported but not confirmed, that he would encourage the troopers to rape women and girls in front their families. He became so powerful that some of the German officers handled him with care."

"Pierre instigated the storming of two Jewish homes, the male members of the families were shot and the females were taken away destined for one of the concentration camps. He then removed all the valuable paintings and silverware from the house and then plundered the Picture Gallery belonging to one member of the family stealing all the paintings, which, he stored until after the war along with the contents of several more Galleries, which he had stolen and shot the owners after torturing them to obtain their Swiss Bank account number. This man now owns two exclusive Galleries in Paris and he is so wealthy that no one suspects his past. That gentlemen is the dossier on Pierrer Ingle, I think you will agree with me, when I say, he is an ideal candidate for our first elimination."

He produced a little black bag.

"In this bag are six slips of paper, on one slip is a large red cross, who ever takes this slip out of the bag is the one to deal with the elimination of Pierre Ingle."

"Whoever pulls out this slip must treat it with the utmost confidence; no one must know who has drawn the slip, agreed?" They all nodded.

"When this matter has been dealt with, I want an announcement put in the personal column of the English Telegraph Newspaper, saying,

A sudden death has occurred in the Smith family while on holiday in Brighton and we will all know the execution has been carried out and you will be notified about our next meeting."

"How do you feel about the situation Nathan?"

"Peter and I voted to go with the proposition, so we must go along with it."

*

Françoise Flowers left the meeting feeling very desperate; he had committed himself to kill a human being, something he had never done before, never ever thought about doing. Quite recently, he had paid a man to kill one of his racing pigeons that had broken its wing.

He arrived home and he felt shattered, he went straight to his room and took a hot shower. Having got dressed he went downstairs to join his wife for a meal.

"What is wrong Françoise, you look quite ill, I do hope you are not going down with a cold?"

"The meeting was very hectic and in many ways upsetting."

When the meal was over, he went into the conservatory and sat in his favourite chair but suddenly he felt as if his stomach had fallen down into his boots. He suddenly realized that agreeing to something and now faced with having to carry out to what he agreed, is something entirely different. How on earth can I bring myself to carry out this mission? He decided it would have to be a tragic accident; I cannot possibly kill with my own hand. He realized he would have to give this matter a lot of thought, even if it means enlisting the help of his deputy.

Yes, I will discuss this with my senior intelligence officer. I feel confident he is trustworthy and he has a score to settle with people like Ingle, his grandparents were shot for helping a Free French pilot who had been shot down while operating from an airfield in England during the war, a person similar to Pierre Ingle had informed on them.

*

The following morning, Françoise opened up his office, after dealing with his mail; he telephoned Jacque asking him to come to his office.

When he entered the office Françoise told him that he wanted to speak to him in the strictest confidence, to prevent anyone overhearing our conversation we will go for a walk in the park, Françoise turned to Jacque.

"Have you got your phone with you?"

"No"

"Good".

Françoise then briefly outlined the finding of the envelope and what had been the outcome on its contents.

"I have drawn the short straw to eliminate Pierre Ingle."

"My god, he is a very influential person.

He is known throughout the area for his impeccable dress and his black patent shining shoes and the bright coloured bow tie he wears, it is so colourful; so bright, like a searchlight on a dark night."

Jacque's face changed completely as Françoise told him about the dossier that is the type of man he has been.

"I have given you all the information but it must remain with you."

"Now, can I rely on your help?"

"You most certainly can, it was a person such as he that got my grandparents killed."

"We will have to set out a plan, which will work without leaving any doubt that it was a tragic accident, or the death was carried out by an operating Jewish group, in revenge for their relatives deaths for which he was responsible. The options are shooting, poison or a tragic accident, shall we think about it for a couple of days?"

"Jacque, will you shadow Pierre and then we can build up a picture of his daily routine? When you think you have established a pattern, call into my office, thanks Jacque?"

Several days later Françoise received a phone call from Jacque, asking if he could call that morning to discuss their latest project.

His immediate response was yes; do come this morning, he was still very anxious about his task.

When Jacque arrived at Françoise offices, he was shown into a small private room; obviously it had been swept on a regular basis to ensure that there were no bugs or any listening devices in operation.

Francoise poured out two glasses of Cognac, handing one to Jacque.

"What have you to report?"

"I have been shadowing Pierre for several days and his daily pattern is that each day during the week he goes for lunch to a small but very expensive restaurant just off the Champs-Elysées.

I am told that he has his own bottles of wine kept there for his private use.

How do I know this? My cousin is the Maitre-de at this restaurant. He being my cousin, we shared the same grandparents and he is prepared to help, your name has not been mentioned at all Francoise, you have no need to worry. The only thing I want from you is a phial of poison, the slow acting poison the type we have used before."

"I will have it here for you tomorrow morning."

"My cousin will add the poison to Pierre's wine when the opportunity presents itself; I am unable to tell you when this will happen, Alonzo must be very careful."

Eight days later Françoise's secretary brought his morning coffee into his office and she laid the morning newspaper on his desk. On the second page of the newspaper was a report that a prominent Art Dealer had suffered a massive heart attack in his office. The hospital tried to revive him but the attack had been so severe that he had died.

Jacque called later that morning to discuss any further instructions for him to carry out. Francoise pointed at the newspaper article.

"A good piece of work, the draught reacted very well with it having the delayed action, it allowed him to get away from the restaurant. I am indebted to you Jacque."

They shook hands and Jacque left the office.

Françoise being a very senior Government official, his job was to prevent crime; his action has made him feel uncomfortable.

The next duty Francoise had to perform was to arrange for a report to be inserted in the Personal Column in the British Telegraph Newspaper and wait for the next meeting in Paris.

That evening, a small village situated between Rouen and Paris decided to have a party after reading the newspaper, not to celebrate Pierre Ingles life but his death. He was responsible for having twenty young people from the village shot during the German occupation.

When his funeral took place, it was reported in the newspaper there were very few mourners but six of the mourners were the same names as on the list.

Francoise attended the funeral and Pierre's wife, daughter and grandchildren were on the front row in tears, Francoise felt pangs of guilt but thinking about the misery Pierre had caused for so many families, it washed away his feelings of guilt.

CHAPTER 2

Three days later Nathan, Home Secretary and Peter Horne MP, received a phone call asking them to attend a meeting in Paris. When the meeting was convened the chairman told the meeting that the first named person had been eliminated and whoever had been responsible, had executed the job very professionally.

That person won't be expected to undertake the next name to be eliminated.

I have six playing cards, I will deal each one of you a card and the one who receives the Ace of Spade is responsible for the next elimination, again, when this has been carried out place the notice in the Telegraph Newspaper.

Each person sat around the table a little on edge, François smiled when he picked up his card and it was a Joker. The chairman had said it would all be very confidential but Françoise felt sure he knew.

Looking around the table, one man's face told it was he to carry out the killing.

Now gentlemen, I have the nine remaining names in this small black bag, pointing to the second man sitting at the table, please take a name from the bag. He pulled out a slip of paper and handed it to the chairman Jan Krupp.

"The person to be dealt with is Otto Speirs, he is the younger brother of Heine and he is even more vicious than his brother.

The chairman went to his brief case and pulled out a folder labelled Otto Speirs.

"This man was delegated the job of setting up the concentration camps, his first camp was to accommodate 5000 Jews and he designed the delousing shower units and they were built by slave labour in the prison camp.

As you're all aware the showers were in fact gas chambers. A batch of the prisoners consisting of men, women and children were made to strip and enter the showers to get rid of the lice but the guards would bolt the doors and turn on the gas, when this happened there would be screaming, wailing and shouting, the noise gradually quietened down and eventually stopped, they were all dead.

A group of prisoners referred to as trustees would man handle the bodies and drag them into a large ditch, before the lime was poured over them, gold teeth and any jewellery the women had hidden in their mouths would be collected, bagged and handed into the office, the added value amounted to an immense fortune. The so-called trustees knew if they spoke about removing the bodies, they would be included be in the next batch."

*

"Otto was listed to appear at the Nuremberg war crimes trials but he was smuggled out of Germany and he is living in Brazil as a family man. He married into a prominent wealthy family and they have four children and the house is guarded 24 hours each day.

He receives a substantial monthly income, from where or from whom we are unable to trace the source. The number of atrocities carried out by Otto are too numerous to list. The vile man would boast that the beautiful green grass in the large meadows surrounding the camp was due to it being fed with Jewish bone meal. Whoever has drawn the task of eliminating Otto? Must be very careful, for some reason he is still well guarded."

Nathan had drawn the Black Ace; it was up to him to eliminate Otto but he couldn't take his wife Olga with him to Brazil. If it became necessary for him to go to Brazil he would have to concoct a story, if she knew his real reason she would be very angry and fearful for his life. He realized that this was going to be a very dangerous assignment.

On his return, he called his most senior intelligence men Ken Lee and Major Lance Goodchild to his office. They sat down and Nathan explained the task he had to perform, when he had finished going through the details. Ken suggested that he would send two of his most senior men to Brazil to complete a dossier on Otto, before making any move.

"We should know the location where he is living and all about his daily activities, even what he eats for breakfast." Nathan and Lance agreed that would be a very sensible approach to make. When Ken returned to his office, he asked his secretary, to bring him the files of his senior agents who have had experience abroad recently. After going through the files, he decided on Brian Lowe and Gordon Wentworth, they both being very experienced agents.

*

Brian and Gordon met up at Heathrow Airport, they had not worked together for a year or so and they had a lot of catching up to do. Their flight had been booked for them and they were flying into Brasillia International Airport, this being the third largest Airport, their bosses thought this would be safer.

However, on landing they were interrogated as to the purpose of their visit to Brazil, was it business or pleasure? The reason given for their visit, was to help Gordon convalesce after a long serious illness, the reason was accepted.

They caught a taxi to the hotel that had been booked for their stay, when they went to the reception desk they had to surrender their passports, which, is the normal procedure. Brian queried the fact with the man on the desk that they should keep their passports, as they would need them to change Sterling to the local currency, he was told not to worry as he could obtain change at the hotel.

They were shown to their rooms, they decided to take a shower, a change of clothing and then go out for a meal, after the meal they went to several café bars asking questions, hoping to locate Otto's locality.

They gleaned a little knowledge but not the answers they were hoping for, they spent the next three days visiting the various bars asking questions.

On the fourth morning they went to a coffee bar and sat at a table on the pavement, Brian, was becoming very despondent, in spite of his experience in the field, he was getting nowhere.

As they stood up to leave the café, a large black limousine pulled up along side of them, three burly men got out and pushed them into the back of the car and it sped off.

"What the hell do you think you are doing?" Gordon asked.

"Shut up."

The car pulled off the main road to join a long driveway leading to a large house. The car came to a halt outside the main door, two men came out and ushered them inside the house. They were taken into a room and left.

Gordon looked at Brian,

"What the hell is going on?" Brian shrugged his shoulders.

The door opened, a small well-dressed gentleman entered the room.

"Good afternoon gentlemen, I hope my boys were not too rough with you. Would you care for a glass of wine or iced water?" they asked for water, he nodded to the man who had followed him into the room. The man returned with a tray with three glasses and a glass jug of water.

"Just before I give you this water, he poured out some water from the jug into one glass and proceeded to drink it. Just to show you the water is not drugged or anything silly."

He then poured out the water for Gordon and Brian. When they had finished drinking the water, the man turned to Brian.

"Now will you answer my question?"

"Why are you in Brazil?"

"Gordon is here to convalesce after suffering a serious illness."

"Why are you going around and asking so many questions?"

"I have been told all of your questions appear to be centred on the location of Otto Speirs, he escaped from Germany when the Third Reich collapsed.

If you level with me, I might be able to help you;

If necessary I can destroy you. Just give this matter some serious thought; I want to know your interest in Otto.

My boys will now take you back to your hotel, tomorrow morning meet me for coffee at 10.30."

He handed Brian a card showing the name and position of the café bar. He shook hands saying.

"Good day gentlemen, I look forward to meeting you tomorrow morning."

When they got back in their hotel room Gordon said.

"Shall we leave the country or meet him for coffee in the morning? If we do return home we will have failed our mission. Let us chance it; we will keep the appointment in the morning.

Brian, we have been in tighter situations than this before now."

The following morning after breakfast Gordon and Brian relaxed in the lounge reading an English newspaper; Gordon looked at his watch and suggested they should get ready to go out and keep the appointment.

They arrived bang on time, the man was already there and a pot of coffee and three cognacs were on the table.

He stood up to shake hands.

"Good morning gentlemen, I hope you will enjoy the cognacs." All three sat enjoying their drinks.

He looked at them through his steel rimmed spectacles with a fixed grin on his face.

"Gentlemen, let us stop playing games, I know you are Brian Lowe and you are Gordon Wentworth, you are both British intelligence agents and your boss is Nathan and why you are here? I am Colonel Black head of the Zionist Secret Service but from now on I am Bernie to you, Okay? We have spent almost a year locating Otto Speirs and we have invested a lot of our time, making plans to take our revenge on this man. You two have been going around asking questions about Otto and this will filter back to him and he will raise his guard."

"I am not asking but telling you to back off, if you don't, you will be dealt with, which would distress me."

"I can give you a copy of Otto's address, his hobbies, eating habits, his family, girlfriend and even down to the toiletries he uses. The report is so comprehensive; it even tells how many times he uses the toilet, daytime and night time. Would that copy satisfy you?"

"Colonel, it would be great, that is what we came for, to compile a dossier."

"Otto's main hobby is diving searching for wrecks on the sea bed; confidentially, it is his oxygen tanks we are focusing our attention on.

If you would like to enjoy your stay and keep your nose out of our business, you can return to Nathan armed with the dossier you came for and a copy of Otto's death certificate. I have shown complete trust in you both, now you must respect me."

*

Five days later, the man on the reception desk handed Brian an envelope, it was an invitation to join Colonel Black and his wife for dinner. Brian rang and accepted the invitation.

They went by taxi to the address shown in the letter. Bernie's wife, Lottie was absolutely charming and the meal was most enjoyable. The conversation was mainly about their stay in Brazil and their home and family, who they are hoping to meet in two days time when they arrive back home. His wife said.

"Now the conferences Bernie had to attend are now finalized, we can go home."

Bernie called his car round to the front of the house; they said good-byes and left to return to their hotel, as they were leaving Bernie handed Gordon an envelope.

It was as promised, a comprehensive dossier on Otto Speirs and attached to the last copy was a copy of his death certificate there was a newspaper cutting reporting on Otto's death, his breathing apparatus failed while diving too deep, he was suffocated, written underneath in ink, "As were those in the gas chamber."

*

The following morning they visited the British Embassy, they were introduced to the members of the staff and when they said they wanted to send a report, they were taken to the secrets room. The report was coded and dispatched.

They both felt happier when this had been dispatched. They intended flying home the following day and they were concerned should the envelope be removed while their bags were being examined.

When they arrived home and visited Nathan's office, they found him so excited. He congratulated them on such a professional job and promised a substantial bonus. Brian looked at Gordon and smiled but neither commented from where the report came or who engineered Otto's death. When they left his office, Nathan contacted the Telegraph Newspaper to insert a piece in the personal column.

CHAPTER 3

Nathan and Peter were notified of the next meeting, which, was to be held in Paris. On arrival, they all filed into the room and claimed their allocated seats.

The Chairman, Jan Krupp stood up.

"Thank you gentlemen for coming along, no doubt you will have read of the sad loss in the Smith family. I will deal the cards as the last time and the member who is dealt the Ace of Spades has the duty to perform the next elimination."

Françoise picked up his card, he breathed a sigh of relief, it was the Joker and Nathan hesitated before he picked up his card and he lifted the corner and relaxed, it was the two of clubs. Looking round the table it was obvious by the look on Boris Bormann's face; it was he that had been dealt the card to perform the elimination.

Boris held a very important position in the German Government; he wondered what his superiors would think of him attending this meeting and now his duty.

The chairman had put the remaining eight names in the little black bag, he pointed to the third man down the table, kindly select a name from this bag. The man pulled out a slip of paper and handed it to the Chairman.

"The next gentleman selected is an Englishman, Robin Grenfell, he left Britain in 1938 to join the Nazi party in Germany; he was sadly missed by the London group of Black shirts.

He being a doctor, he was given the job of setting up the various medical centres within the concentration camps.

During the war, the prisoners would be bled to help the wounded German soldiers but with one stipulation, which, was no Jewish blood was to be used but when things got desperate it was.

Medical experiments would be carried out on the female prisoners and this often resulted in badly deformed children being born and in many cases the women would die but this did not stop them. One of the main experiments was to castrate the men and sterilize the women and then carry out an experiment attempting to reverse the operation.

The idea was mooted, this would enable the authorities to control birth and ensure only a pure German race existed. There was one case of using a University Professor, to test a serum injection; it reduced the man to a blithering idiot in twelve hours.

The pain and misery Robin Grenfell inflicted on humanity should have put him on trial in Nuremberg but he escaped justice by fleeing to Switzerland. He is now a well-respected cosmetic surgeon and a very wealthy member of their society. His patients would shudder, if they knew how he had gained his knowledge of dealing with skin."

Boris called five of his most trusted members of his team to a meeting in his office. He outlined the duty he had to perform and it was decided to dispatch one member to gain a complete picture of Robin's daily and weekly routine, even down to how many times he blows his nose each day, one member giggled but Boris slapped him down, that is how serious this project is. Boris called another meeting when the man returned with the details he had asked for.

"I am just a little concerned; Robin must be a little bothered, seeing two of his group meeting up with an accident, which cost them their lives. He has had bulletproof tyres and proofed windows fitted on the driver's side of his car. He is most vulnerable on a Wednesday afternoon when he drives through the St Gothard Tunnel; I had toyed with the idea of shooting his tyres but now it would be of no use."

Another member of the team, Karl Frick said.

"We will have to resort to a plan we have used in the past. Remove the tyre valve; pour some explosive liquid into both front tyres, before we put the valve back, attach a small detonator at the bottom of the valve, which, we can control with a hand held monitor and if he speeds like the rest of the traffic in the tunnel, it will be easy, we can activate the liquid explosive on the left hand front wheel.

All it will do is to blow the tyre off the wheel rim, exploding the second tyre a few seconds after the first, this should result in the complete loss of control of the steering and he will crash into a concrete stanchion or the wall."

"The impact should shred the tyres but in any case, the explosive liquid does not leave any stain and the detonator is only one eighth the size of a small aspirin, which will disintegrate with the heat of the explosion, in fact, it will deny any accident investigation result."

"What you are saying, if we can't puncture the tyre from the outside, we go inside?"

"Yes, I am sure it will work, providing he travels at his normal speed. The average traffic speed through the tunnel is normally seventy miles an hour."

Another member joined in.

"As previously mentioned, this method has been used before. In any case, the man operating the hand held monitor would be first on the scene of the accident."

*

Agent Ernst Raeder offered to go to Basle and arrange a meeting with one of their agents.

"Are you sure the hand held monitor will operate in such an enclosed area as a tunnel?"

"Yes, I have carried out several tests, my radio continues to play and I have a signal on my radio telephone."

Boris turned to Ernst.

"Whatever you need, will be made available, just give one days notice."

"Boris, will you check how long the liquid is stable?"

"Yes, I will, we don't want to kill the wrong man," said Boris laughing.

On arrival to Basle, Ernst contacted their agent named Paul and explained the reason for his visit.

He asked him to find the garage where Robin's car is parked overnight.

"We will need an engineer to carry out injecting the liquid and re-inflating the tyres, I have money available."

Paul looked at Ernst.

"I'll ring your hotel room with this information. I know just the man for this job, expensive but thorough and dependable but don't ask his name, he won't tell you."

Ernst booked into his hotel and went to his room, as he opened his door the phone started to ring.

Without any preliminaries, the voice said,

"Meet me in our usual bar at eight o'clock" and put the phone down."

Ernst had a meal in the hotel and relaxed in the lounge with his coffee, looking at his watch he decided to have a steady stroll to the café bar to meet Paul.

When he approached the table Paul stood up and greeted Ernst as long lost friend.

"The man wants 2000Frs for the use of the garage where Robin's car is parked and a further 1000 to deal with the job.

If you agree, he can carry it out on Monday night?"

"Right Paul, arrange it for Monday night, shall I give you the money now, or leave it until Monday night?"

"Leave it until Monday Ernst."

"One other thing Paul, can you get me a plan showing where the emergency exit stairs from the tunnel are situated in case of an accident or fire, please?"

Monday night Ernst began feeling a little jumpy, hoping everything will go well. Paul met Ernst and took him to the garage, the mechanic had removed the valve centres and injected the liquid into the tyres and Ernst gave him the small detonators, which he attached to the bottom of the valve and they were screwed back in place, he started to inflate the tyres very, very slowly, not to create heat. Knowing the mechanic would not respond to any name.

"Mr. Mechanic, there is the money you wanted, just one other thing, would it be possible for you to put a different colour bulb on the drivers side small light. It will help with my identification, putting his car apart from the other traffic?"

"I can do that for you sir but you will have to pay for the bulb?"

"Certainly, will another five francs do?"

"Thanks."

Ernst took Paul to one side.

"Everything appears to be okay, I have paid him, when he has put the coloured side light bulb in I think we will leave. That is phase one completed; we must now keep our fingers crossed."

*

Tuesday, Paul and Ernst met up for lunch, during lunch Paul passed a copy of the stairway escape route across the table to Ernst, as he had asked for.

"There is one problem; the doors will only open outwards coming up the stairs from the tunnel, not, decending from the pavement, that is, without these two keys." Paul pushed the keys across the table, smiling.

"After lunch, shall we investigate?"

"Yes, I think we should."

When they had finished their lunch, they strolled along the pavement, eventually they came to a small brick building with an exit door, according to the plan this must be the one.

They stopped, looking around Ernst turned the key and they quickly went through the door. The passage leading down the stairs was illuminated.

They very carefully went down the stairs the second key opened the door into the tunnel. The echo of the traffic noise made it impossible to speak to each other.

Ernst was very pleased, he had a clear view of the approaching traffic and the odd coloured lights would help him to identify Robin's car.

They decided to leave the tunnel. They did not need the keys as the emergency bars opened the doors going up.

According to the previous surveillance, Robin leaves the garage at eleven o'clock on the Wednesday morning travelling to meet his young lady for lunch.

The following morning at ten thirty Ernst had got himself settled in a cavity in the wall of the tunnel, which gave him a clear view of the oncoming traffic.

His main concern had been if the concrete stanchions had been in the way to affect the wireless waves from the hand held monitor.

He sat watching the traffic his eyes started playing tricks in the dimly lit tunnel.

Then! He saw a car in the distance with odd coloured lights; this must be Grenfell's car, he sat, patiently waiting for the car to get a little closer.

He pressed button one, it worked, the car began to careering side to side and then as he pressed the second button, the car started to spin out of control, hitting the wall at a very high speed with a loud crash. Ernst was staggered, as the car hit the wall it burst into flames and then exploded, Ernst was fifty meters away from the crash and the heat was so intense that he quickly started up the stairs followed by the occupants of other cars.

He walked out on to the pavement, as he was strolling along; he saw ambulances and police cars speeding towards the tunnel entrance with their sirens wailing. He was hoping that he had achieved what he came to Balse for but he would have to wait for the report.

He returned back to his hotel room. He switched on the radio, the crash was being reported but the occupant had yet to be identified due to the intense heat caused by the explosion.

He poured himself out a drink and lay back in his chair and listened to the radio commentator giving out information as he received it. Later that evening, it was announced that the occupant was Robin Grenfell a prominent cosmetic surgeon who had died in the crash.

Boris heard the news later that evening and he then arranged for the loss of another member of the Smith family to be reported in the Telegraph Newspaper.

Jan Krupp had finished reading the article about the loss to the Smith family, a smile crossed his face, smiling he said to himself. "We are getting there."

CHAPTER 4

Peter and Nathan travelled to Paris together to attend the next meeting. On arrival, they were directed to the hotel room, which had been allocated and had been checked by the security people.

When the six ministers were all seated, the Chairman, Count Jan Krupp stood up.

"You will all have read the notice in the Telegraph Newspaper, the Smith family has had another sad loss and a slight smile crossed his face.

You all appear to be comfortable with the card system of selection," they all nodded.

He dealt the six cards around the table; there were audible sighs of relief, as they picked up their card. Peter picked up his card and he felt sick, it was he who had to perform the next elimination.

"Gentlemen, having dealt the cards I will now ask one of you to select a name from this black bag" he pointed to the fourth man down the table.

"Will you do the honours sir?"

He pulled out the slip of paper and handed it to the Chairman.

"The name selected is Alfred Schelling; I will now read out the copy of his dossier.

He was a senior Gestapo Officer; his duty was to visit the Jewish housing area and knocking on the doors to collect donations for the Nazi Party. If the man refused to make a donation, at a later date he would be arrested and taken to the Gestapo Headquarters in the town centre. His wife or family would be asked for a large ransom to be paid for his safe return, if they failed to pay, their husband or family would be returned in a body bag.

After the news had circulated, very few refused to pay. In the case of a young widow who refused or was unable to pay for her father's release; several SS. Troopers were stationed in her house for twenty four hours, which Schelling treated as joke.

In cases where the ransom was paid short, the dead body would arrive home in a bag.

In one case he shot an entire family, just wounding the head of the family; he was tortured until he gave the details of his Swiss bank account and then shot dead. This man is very vicious, whoever has the job of eliminating Schelling must be very careful as he has many influential wealthy friends.

He is now residing in Hastings in the UK, how he was allowed to enter Gt Britain and live there, we shall never know."

The meeting broke up and Peter had to stay in Paris to attend a conference, he said cheerio to Nathan and promised to give him a ring when he returned home.

Several days later Nathan received a phone call from Peter.

"Nathan, may I call round to discuss a delicate matter?"

"Yes, anytime today."

Peter called for his car to pick him up outside his office. He being an MP, he is supplied with a chauffeur- driven car. Peter arrived at Nathan's office buildings; he was shown into his office, they shook hands.

"Peter, did you get the Ace of Spades?"

"Yes, I did and I am at a loss how to deal with it."

"May I suggest, we ask two of our most experienced intelligence officers to call at this office and I am sure they will know what to do?"

"They did a fantastic job for me in Brazil so I can thoroughly recommend them."

Nathan asked his secretary to contact Gordon Wentworth and Brian Lowe to come to this office urgently.

They both arrived half an hour later. Nathan introduced Peter to them, who then spoke to them.

"I would like a complete dossier on Alfred Schelling who is living in Hastings, I have to kill him myself, or arrange for him to meet his death through a tragic accident."

Nathan handed each a slip of signed paper.

"Take this to the cashier and she will give you money to cover your travel and hotel expenses."

*

They spent the first week following Alfred's movements and his hobbies. They discovered his main hobby was fishing, he owns a small seagoing fibre- glass fishing boat. He takes the boat out to sea at least twice a week and he is accompanied with another man; on investigation we find it is an old friend from his village in Germany.

Having got his personal information, they made a point of viewing the house in which he is living. The following day they wandered around the

Marina where Alfred had his boat moored, his boat was pointed out to them by another boat owner who was working on his boat.

They casually walked along the pontoons and looked at Alfred's fishing boat. Gordon spotted that the boat was fitted out with living quarters and by looking through the small cabin window, he could see a gas ring and a small oven. The gas supply was supplied from a calor gas cylinder, which, was in a metal frame bolted on the after deck.

Gordon's mind started ticking over.

The next day they went back to London and visited Peter, as they walked into his office, Brian put his fingers to his lips, indicating, Can we talk?

"Yes Brian, this office is swept daily for any listening devices."

"Right, we have a complete dossier on Alfred and Gordon has come up with a brilliant idea, would you like to hear it?"

"Indeed I would."

"The gas for the domestic area is supplied from a calor gas canister on the after deck and this is what feeds the gas oven and ring. The pipes from the canister are plastic and they run under the deck boards to the gas oven. The evening before he goes out sea fishing, we will drill several small holes in the plastic pipes allowing the gas to seep into the bilges and put a small explosive near the holes. When they arrive at their fishing area, they are sure to make a cup of tea or coffee. When they strike a match to light the ring, the gas in the bilges will ignite and should be, Good Bye Alfred."

"The plan sounds good but how will you manage to get on to the boat the night before unseen?"

"There are so many men wandering about and watching others messing about on their boats doing odd jobs, another two won't be noticed."

"I always thought gas would enter the atmosphere, how come it will remain in the bilges?"

"Calor gas is a domestic gas supplied in portable cylinders and consists of butane liquefied under pressure; the liquid will stay in the bilges. It will be dealt with but we can't give you a timetable. At the present time, we are trying to find out the date when the next sea rod competition is to take place. They usually stay at sea for a couple of days, maybe more." Peter stood up.

"Thank you gentlemen, I will leave it with you and good luck, the bonus payments will be good."

Gordon decided to go ahead that evening but he asked Brian not to go along with him, "I will not be noticed by myself if I mingle with the other boat people."

"Okay Gordon, if that is the way you want to play it, just phone me if you should need help at all."

Brian was not really concerned, as he felt sure that Gordon knew exactly how he was going to deal with the gas pipes.

The following morning Brian rang Gordon's home telephone number, his wife Ruth answered the phone.

"Good morning Ruth, may I speak to Gordon?"

"He is not at home Brian; he did not come home last night perhaps he has been sent out of town."

"Okay Ruth, I will catch him later."

Brian kept his voice on a level tone but he was quite worried, he decided to go down to the Marina and look around. He strolled along the pontoon to check on Alfred's boat but there was no activity on his, or any of the surrounding boats.

I will leave it a few days before I start enquiring just in case he has been given another job to do.

*

Jan Krupp was sat reading his newspaper but his eyes started to close, As he put his newspaper down, his phone started to ring.

"Hello, Jan Krupp here."

"Hello Jan, this is a voice from the past, this is Karl Jodl, would you mind coming to my Berlin office?"

"Not at all Karl, it is a long time since we last met up, in fact, I should be congratulating you on your promotion. Two days time okay?

That will give me a chance, to catch upon some paperwork before I leave my office?"

Jan asked his secretary to book him into a hotel, on the outskirts of Berlin. He thought the city would be far too busy by the time he would arrive on Wednesday evening.

He left his office at five thirty, he could have kicked himself, he had chosen the busiest time of the day to travel. He was pleased that he had decided to stay outside the city of Berlin.

He was delighted with the choice of hotel his secretary had made, before going down for dinner he visited the leisure area and enjoyed a swim and a sauna. Why haven't I done this before, instead of just, work, work and still more work, it is about time I started to enjoy myself again. He went up to his room and got dressed for dinner.

Sitting at the dinner table, again he was mentally congratulating his secretary as the choice of food from the menu was fantastic, also the wine list. He went back to his room feeling absolutely marvellous; he decided he should ring his wife to tell her of his safe arrival.

*

The next morning he was up early and enjoyed a good breakfast, he was looking forward to meeting Karl again. It is a number of years since they last worked together; it was during the difficult years just after the war. Jan rescued Karl from the Russians in Eastern Berlin, for which, Karl has always been grateful.

Jan checked out of his room and drove his car to keep the appointment in Berlin; he pulled up outside the building, as he walked towards the reception desk, he was approached by a young man.

"Sorry sir, you cannot park your car outside this building, that is the rule."

"How long has that rule been in force?"

"Three months, sir."

"Have you an appointment here sir?"

"Yes, I am here to visit Karl Jodl."

"In that case sir, give Rudolf your car key and he will park your car, just ring down when you are ready to leave and he will bring your car to the front of the building for you."

"Thank you, that is very kind."

The man on the reception desk beckoned a uniformed young man.

"Take this gentleman to Mr. Karl Jodl's office."

Jan followed the guide along the corridor, eventually, he stopped at a door and knocked, Jan heard someone call.

"Enter"

Jan walked in, Karl stood up.

"Hello, Jan, my very good friend."

Jan sat down and looked around the office; it was still as elegant as he remembered it, even the light from the beautiful cut glass chandelier was still glistening on all the highly polished wooden panelled walls and desk. The only thing that was different was the Nazi insignia had been removed from the wall behind the desk and a picture of the German Eagle was hanging in its place.

Karl pressed a button on his desk and a young lady brought coffee and biscuits into the office and placed the tray on the desk.

"Jan, no doubt, you are wondering the reason I asked you to visit, I have job for you.

The reason I have selected you is because you are away from all the people spreading rumours in Berlin.

Let us enjoy the coffee and catch up on our families."

They spent the next half an hour discussing their home life.

"I want you and your team to concentrate on tracing a group of vigilantes, they are tracking down and eliminating Ex Nazi personnel, whom they considered to have carried out atrocities during the war but escaped abroad and not brought to face justice in Nuremberg.

The rumour says this is a list of twenty people who we consider might be under threat, three of the people on the list have already been killed their names are underlined with black ink on the copy of the list I will give you.

We may be wrong, it could be a Jewish group operating from outside Europe. There is a rumour going around that the list of names to be eliminated was found in an old cinema in Liverpool, it may be so but I just don't know Jan."

"It is not just a rumour about the list Jan, what I have given you is a copy of the list but that is confidential. If we told how we came in possession of that list, it would put our agent in danger."

Jan sat inwardly laughing to himself, he could give his friend the information he wanted but he wasn't going to.

How has it become public knowledge, surely none of those present at the meetings would let it leak.

"Give this matter your urgent attention Jan, you can phone me anytime but use this number shown on this card."

"Karl, will ask your young lady to ring down and ask Rudolf to bring my car round to the main entrance."

They both stood up and Karl looked at Jan.

"The years are treating you well Jan"

They shook hands and Jan was just about to leave, there was a terrific explosion, they both rushed downstairs.

"It was your car that has blown up Mr. Krupp and Rudolf was driving."

"My god Jan, who knew you were coming here?"

"No one, as I am aware Karl."

I do hope I have not put you in the firing line for the vigilantes Jan?"

"Maybe just a warning shot, to convince me to mind my own business."

Jan decided not to make any further comments but how did the bomber know what he was here for, or have they traced him as the Chairman of the vigilantes. I will ask the people who has carried out the eliminations to break cover and I can investigate the remaining three, no; there could be only two by the end of the week and the remaining four we will have to arrange. I will consider my next move very carefully.

"I will get a car brought out from the car pool for you to drive home." They shook hands again and Karl went back to his office.

Jan went to reception desk to say how sorry he was that Rudolf had been killed, because he felt that he was responsible.

The man on the desk said.

"This has become a regular occurrence over the past few weeks sir. I have no idea why these people should try and disrupt our daily life. We are all working for a living, trying to build a better life for our families, very few people are interested in politics and the politicians have caused enough damage to the average man to last his life time."

*

A car was brought round to front of the building and the keys were handed to Jan.

"Have a safe journey sir." Jan just smiled,

"Thanks, I hope so too."

He was pleased when he did arrive home; He had found that his car being blown up had unnerved him. If it had been him that had collected his car, it would be his body parts that had been collected up and taken to the mortuary.

As he entered his house, his wife, Lauren, knew something was wrong. He told her what had happened earlier and she too was very upset.

"Ho! Dear Jan, I do hope we are not going back to those bad old dark days."

That evening, he spent some time working in his study. He spent the time arranging the next meeting but he decided to change the venue to

Cologne and they were told to hand their cars over to one of his men who will be on hand. The man will stay with the car until the minister leaves, just as a matter of security.

The six intelligence officers arrived and when then all got settled in their allocated seat.

Jan stood up.

"Gentlemen, I am sorry to tell you, we have had our operation leaked to the authorities. Last Wednesday I was called to Berlin by Karl Jodl, he instructed me to trace the vigilantes who are tracking down and eliminating Ex Nazi officers. All those present chuckled, including Jan.

When I arrived at the building, I was told that I was not allowed to park my car outside the building; a young man took my keys and parked the car for me. When he got into the car to bring it out of the car park, he turned the ignition key and the car exploded. Obviously that was intended for me, how anyone knew I was going to this meeting is anyone's guess.

The disturbing fact is we have a mole in our midst. Karl even knew about the envelope being found in Liverpool and he has a copy and he has given me a copy. Whoever, is dealing with the elimination number four, I suggest you hang fire for a while, let them think the warning they gave me has changed our minds. I am not accusing any one of you in this room but somehow our intentions have become known to the very people we are attacking.

In view of what happened to my car, your cars are being protected by my team so you can feel comfortable. That is the reason for my calling you here today, to advise you watch your backs. Now, I have arranged for a meal to be served in this room, eat drink and be merry, as the saying goes. Gentlemen, please be careful."

They all began chatting to each other, at least the ones who could understand the languages but each had a way of being understood.

Nathan turned to Peter Horn.

"How far has your arrangements gone Peter?"

"As far as I know, everything is being prepared, now, in view of what the Chairman has told us, do we strike now or wait a while?"

"That is a difficult one Peter; if you wait, they might have raised their guard.

May I suggest you discuss it with the operators, it all depends how far the plans have progressed."

"Yes, Nathan I will do that, to be fair, it is they who are risking their lives."

The Chairman approached Nathan.

"Have you any thoughts on who is taking us on?"

"Jan, if one of my senior men, Major Lance Goodchild was asked that question, he would immediately say Klaus Gunter, he chaired the meeting in Dusseldorf in 1939 and we had a lot of trouble from him during the "Fifth Column" operation in Liverpool when they were looking for something, which turned out to be the envelope we found in the old cinema, during that operation seven men lost their lives. He allows nothing to stand in his way."

"He would probably be right, cheers and do be extra careful."

*

Several days later Brian telephoned Nathan asking if he could visit.

"Certainly Brian, make at three this afternoon, will the time suit you?"

"Thank you sir, I will see you at three."

Brian knocked on Nathan's office door.

"Come in."

"Hello Brian, how can I help you?"

"Have you or any of your officers, sent Gordon out of town on a job?"

"I will ask my secretary to check around, while she is doing that, would you care for a coffee?"

"Yes please, I am very concerned for Gordon's safety."

"We left Peter's office one day last week, after outlining our plans. Gordon decided to deal with matter that evening but did not want me to go with him; his thinking was one person messing about on Alfred's boat would not be as noticeable as two.

Since that day, I have not seen or heard from him, his wife thinks he must be out of town on a job?"

His secretary came into his office.

"Gordon Wentworth is still on a special assignment for Mr.Peter. Horn but he has not heard from him."

"Thanks Gertrude."

Nathan looked at Brian.

"Don't sound too good Brian. Drink your coffee and I will contact all our people around the south coast."

"Did you check on the boat, is it still at its mooring?"

"Yes, I checked when his wife told me he had not been home that night and there was no evidence of anything being out of the ordinary, one thing has just struck me, a padlock was on the cabin door, which I hadn't noticed before."

Nathan's phone rang, he picked up the receiver,

"Put him through Gert."

"Thank you for phoning me, I will be with you in about an hour."

"A body was found on the beach at Bexhill yesterday, our people there appears to think the description fits Gordon. I hope to goodness they are wrong. We will use your car, you know the way."

On arrival at the Bexhill mortuary, they were greeted by a senior intelligence officer and he took them straight to the room to view the body.

Brian took one look.

"Yes, that is Gordon; it looks as if he was garrotted."

"That is what the pathologist has entered on the death certificate."

Nathan turned to the officer.

"Will you arrange for the body to be sent to the mortuary at our special department in London?"

"It will be dealt with today."

"Many thanks for your cooperation."

Brian was very upset,

"I should have gone with him and I could have helped."

"Or, we could have lost two of our senior men. No Brian, they must have been waiting for him, Gordon was a very strong man, so there must have been more than one to overpower him."

"Would you like me to tell his wife Ruth?"

"Yes Brian, you know his wife, we will take care of the funeral expenses. Find out how she would like the funeral conducted and the undertaker she would prefer. Arrange a reception for the guests after the funeral, do not skimp it in any way and tell her to send me the invoice."

*

That evening Brian went round to Ruth's address, he rang the door bell and when she opened the door, she looked at Brian.

"No, please no, is he badly hurt Brian?"

"Come inside."

"Ruth, you must sit down."

"Gordon was killed while on duty, by whom or where we don't know."

At this stage Ruth broke down with tears streaming down her face.

"I will phone your sister Stacey," which he did and Stacey was in the house in five minutes.

Stacey did her best to console Ruth but she was very upset. Her sister made a cup of tea and between Ruth's sobs; Brian explained that whatever funeral plans she made, his boss would meet the expenses.

Stacey and Ruth decided on which Funeral Director they would like to make all the arrangements.

They made the phone call and they were given the date and time.

Brian too, was still very upset, he decided to go home.

Ruth thanked him for coming to tell her of Gordon's death, rather than her being told by a stranger.

Brian and his wife Beryl attended the funeral, he was very surprised by the number of people in the chapel at the crematorium. The service was very well conducted, Gordon was referred to as a civil servant and the way he met his sudden death was not mentioned.

An announcement was made, inviting the mourners to a particular hotel where refreshments will be served. The buffet was quite a lavish affair which pleased Brian and he was amazed how many of the people present he knew.

Having selected some food from the table and drinks from the bar, he led his wife to a small table near a window overlooking a beautiful golf course.

They were chatting away, Ruth walked across to thank Brian for his help, naturally he stood up, suddenly he felt a tap on his shoulder and a voice said,

"Will you introduce me to Ruth?"

"Ruth this Colonel Black."

"I am very pleased to meet you Ruth, I met Gordon on many occasion and I liked him very much, I am very sad this happened, incidentally, my name is Bernie, I came here to offer my condolences, I had every respect for your young man but I am sorry to meet you under such tragic circumstances."

He turned to walk away pulling Brian to go with him.

"We saw what happened but we were too late to prevent it, they put Gordon on a dinghy with an outboard motor, there were four of them holding Gordon. With all the activity, my men finished the job he started; we shall know tomorrow if it works."

"Would you like to meet Nathan and Peter?"

"Yes I would but introduce me as Bernie Black, Okay?"

"Peter and Nathan, may I introduce Bernie Black?"

"I am very pleased to meet you again Bernie." said Nathan.

"We have met before but I was not introduced to you as Bernie Black." They both smiled.

"Brian, my men checked that the pipes had not been corrected early this morning, the fishing competition starts later this evening. Before I go, why do we both keep chasing the same man, perhaps we should join forces."

They strolled out of the hotel, Brian's car was well down the drive, he and Beryl were talking to Bernie and turning to leave, Brian pressed the button on his key pad to release the door lock on his car, the car exploded and was a ball of fire. Everyone was shaken, Nathan sidled up to Brian.

"I think you had better take some time off and go on holiday with your wife."

*

Nathan arrived home still feeling a little uncertain as what was happening, his wife had his dinner ready and he poured out two glasses of wine.

"Cheers Olga," they toasted each other.

The television was on but neither was paying any attention to it but suddenly Nathan pricked up his ears when the newscaster said, "Another fishing boat has been blown up just off the coast at Hastings, it is thought that a World War 11mine had drifted to the surface and caused the explosion."

The government has decided to send a Royal Naval Minesweeping flotilla to carry out a comprehensive sweep, this is the second explosion recently; some quarters think it may be due to the heavy gales, which have broken the rusted mooring cables, which, anchored the old mines to the sea bed.

There were two crew members, one was a well known wealthy Hastings resident named Mr. Alfred. Schelling but the other member we are unable to identify at present. The bodies are being brought ashore on a coastguard boat.

Nathan couldn't help but smile and he felt as if a heavy weight had been lifted from his shoulders. He had just finished his meal when the phone started ringing, his wife picked up the phone.

"Nathan, the call is for you."

"Hello, Nathan here, How are you Peter, are you feeling better?"

"Yes, I heard it too."

"Good, come to my office in the morning and we will discuss it" They were both laughing as they put the phone down.

Nathan suddenly thought, he should not be laughing; a human being has been killed.

Peter called at Nathan's office the following morning.

"Good morning Peter, did you sleep well last night?"

"I did but during the night but I felt uncomfortable when I thought about Gordon and then what could have happened to Brian and his wife, had they been closer to their car. It is getting very nasty."

CHAPTER 5

The small cooling espresso cup sat on the table. Walther Frank looked at it and wondered about a refill. There was a lot to be said about sharpening of the brain that comes with a strong coffee but the jumpiness was something he could do without today.

A copy of the Le Monde Newspaper was folded at the story of Alfred Schelling's death. In isolation the story of Alfred's death was acceptable and believable. Even the story of a death in the St Gothard Pass could be explained away as co-incidental but four deaths in the last fifteen weeks was more than coincidence and an icy chill ran down Walthers back.

It was obvious that a connection between the deaths existed and more worrying the realization that they all belonged on the same list was terrifying, particularly as Walther was without a doubt on the list of people now being slowly wiped out.

Reading of all the newspapers was a routine that had been with Walther for several years now and often it was the smaller headlines which gave the greatest insight in the current political situation.

Only after several attempts at various papers were the entries in the London Telegraph found and when cross- referenced against the dates of the murders it was obvious one group was responsible for the deaths and they were reporting back to each other.

The question was, who would be their next target, how imminent was the threat and how to stop what seemed at the moment to be inevitable.

The large glass window gave a view of Paris from the table with commuters busying their way across the Rue de Boulogne, all enjoying the spring weather but Walther knew that very near the surface of all Parisians was the memory of the occupation by the Germans and the bitterness felt toward those who had been part of the Third Reich or who had collaborated with them. The resentment was often felt more towards the latter than the former.

A hot shower and fresh clothes from the hotel laundry revived Walther's spirits and enabled him to form a plan. He put on a light jacket, not too heavy for the weather but it was loose enough to cover the bulge which would be caused by the Luger 201 strapped to the shoulder holster.

Stepping out on to pavement he hailed a taxi. After a forty minute drive, the taxi drew up at large iron gates with eagles serenely sitting on top of each post straddling the drive. Getting out of the taxi, after leaving a large enough tip to make the driver happy, he started walking up the long drive, each step was filled with caution. He was listening intently for the slightest threatening movement or noise, which years of training had resulted in a professional, who despite several attempts made on his life but was still thankfully alive.

The back door was closed and the large ring door handle groaned at first, then turned and the door opened. Dogs barking loudly seemed to come from another area at the rear of the house then the barking grew louder as three large Doberman dogs flew into the hall. At precisely the same moment a large florid faced man swung round the open door with a revolver in his hand pointing directly at Walther's temple. Without choice he dropped his Luger and stared into the man's eyes, a young lady came running into the room.

"Charlotte, What on earth are you doing here, haven't you been reading the papers?"

He swept his daughter into his arms in a tight embrace.

"I presumed you were abroad with the rest of your Mossad team."

"No dad, on this occasion I'm helping you whether you like it or not. It is about time your secret came out, if only to save your life."

Charlotte waved the man away, he left taking the dogs with him. Walther picked up his Luger and guided Charlotte to a chair and he sat down opposite her.

He looked at his daughter and smiled, "I will tell you all that has happened in my lifetime."

*

"I was born in Austria, this you know as you were born there also, I intend telling you every detail of my life."

"My parents, your grandparents were named Bertha and Louis Collins and they were Jewish. When I was in my teens and the groups of Nazi thugs started terrorizing the Jewish families I decided to change my name from Maurice Collins to Walther Frank. My hair was very light almost blonde and my eyes were not as dark as my parents so I became accepted as from German stock.

He smiled at his daughter; my circumcision was due to a health reason, not religion, I have a letter from a surgeon stating this fact, a

German surgeon, not Jewish, although it was a Rabbi who bought the letter for me."

"Several religious leaders got together and organized and paid to have the basement of this house converted into living and sleeping quarters to house children. The organizing committee consisted of Priests, Vicars, Rabbis and other various religious ministers. It was intended to house children of any denomination if their parents were killed or arrested and transported to Germany to be slave workers.

When the work in the basement had been completed an escape tunnel was constructed leading out through the undergrowth near the river, the river was used to move the children to safety. The first group of children to be brought to the basement was, one Jewish, three Catholics and two Christians, you can see how the religious leaders pooled their resources to benefit the good of all."

*

"I concentrated on warning people, particularly the Jewish families of the likelihood of a visit from the Gestapo. I have been criticized in the past for allowing the death of two, maybe three people in the process of rescuing twenty or thirty very young children.

The Germans gradually accepted me, which enabled me to access a lot of their secret information, which could be used.

The local religious community was aware of my activity and the wealthy business people set me up as being a successful business man. This gave me access to a lot of various meetings with the enemy and I was invited to take part in a planned coup of Europe when Germany was in full control. I was present at the meeting in Dusseldorf in 1939; my name will have been included on the list recently found in Liverpool in the U.K.

I have been playing one against the other for years and I am on the hit list for both parties. I have to tread very carefully and I am constantly looking over my shoulder."

"Dad, I will write up this interview and arrange with the editor to have it included in the local paper, I have a good friend who will deal with the publication."

The interview, not only did it find its way into the local but the national newspapers also. Walther decided to go away for a long holiday to rethink his future, he realized he might get a reprieve from the vigilantes but it might increase the efforts of Klaus Gunter's team to eliminate him from the living.

*

Klaus Gunter arranged a meeting with the remaining five not six of his original team, Walther was not invited. On arrival they all took their allocated seats, when they were all seated, Klaus stood up and looked around at each individual with his bright penetrating eyes, which made some feel uncomfortable.

"Gentlemen, we are in the middle of a war which is being waged against us, we have lost four of our colleagues. I retaliated two weeks ago by having a bomb put in a vigilante's car, hoping that when he turned the key to start the engine, the car would explode but unfortunately a young man, not the owner was killed when he collected the car from the car park. The car belonged to a man who I am convinced is their leader, on this occasion he escaped but I shall keep on trying.

Pierre Ingle, he died from a heart attack but no autopsy ever took place, it was said that the attack was brought on by some drug; how it was administered we cannot say or if our thoughts are correct but I do not believe that he died from natural causes.

Otto Spiers died while diving too deep while looking for old ship wrecks but he was an excellent diver, he was not only an experienced diver but he also taught diving at various depths. Such a man would not go beyond his safe depth and suffocate. He had been living in Brazil for quite a few years and he knew the waters well. We investigated and found that his air tanks had been tampered with but the Brazilian authorities would not pursue with the investigation.

The next loss was Robin Grenfell, here again his death to me was suspect but how the execution was carried out, no one could come up the reason for the crash or if the car had been tampered with but we know it must have been. Robin had taken precautions by having bullet proof tyres and windows fitted.

I was very saddened when I heard that Alfred Schelling had died. We served together on the Russian Front and we were lucky enough to be captured by the Americans, not the Russians.

Prior to Alfred's death we caught a young man tampering with the calor gas pipes on his fishing boat; it was obvious he was planning to destroy the boat and Alfred. My men captured this young man and dealt with him. The annoying thing is Alfred was killed by an old wartime mine rising to the surface and killing him in the explosion. That gentlemen, was the official statement.

Together with our investigating agency, we have published our findings on each of the four deaths. Personally, I don't believe they were accidental; we must take care of each other and be constantly on our guard. If any one of you is able to identify our enemy, contact me immediately and I will deal with that person straight away.

Most of you must have read in the newspapers the situation regarding Walther Frank. It has not yet been decided whether we should deal with him or wait and see what action the other party takes, if they eliminate him it will save us the trouble.

We are very distressed, to think that the list containing the names of the people who attended our meeting in Dusseldorf was found in our 5th Column Station in Liverpool.

Every effort was made to discover where the minutes had been hidden; in fact, two of my friends are serving a prison sentence after being caught while trying to locate the papers. If any one of you thinks that you have come across anything suspicious contact me immediately."

A man known to them all as Bill Funk stood up.

"Klaus, may I meet you in your office when this meeting has closed?"

"Two o'clock, will that time suit you?"

"Thank you, I will be there."

CHAPTER 6

Bill Funk called at Klaus's office as arranged.

Klaus stood up and shook Bill's hand.

"Would you like coffee Bill?"

"Yes please, milk, no sugar."

They sat discussing the general conditions of the European Countries while they were drinking their coffee.

"Now Bill, tell me what is on your mind?"

"I am convinced that the Zionist Chief of Intelligence is Colonel Black and he is cooperating with the vigilantes and the man I am interested in is one of his men, named Isaac Miller. His grandfather and his relatives were heavily involved with the economic war against Germany when Hitler became Chancellor in 1933. This caused catastrophic chaos to the well being of the whole of the German population. His relatives organized and attended the massive anti German rallies in America and England; the outcome of those rallies made the world dramatically reduce trading with Germany. This resulted in mass unemployment and millions living on benefits, just managing to survive.

In Hitler's speeches he urged the German people to boycott the Jewish shops and stores and indicating the tide would turn, which it did."

"Bill, my own family suffered an untold miserable time but we must cast those unpleasant memories to the past."

"Klaus, my grandfather owned and controlled a vast importing and exporting company, exporting food, engineering items, clothing, in fact, what ever a customer asked for he would supply. The Jewish rallies created a world wide impact, his business suffered to such an extent that his business collapsed and he was so devastated that he committed suicide and I blame Isaac Miller's family for his death and I am going to reap my revenge on that man."

"You have my permission to do whatever you wish, if you need any help with money or equipment, just ask. You do realize, I cannot be held responsible for whatever action you decide on, or whatever takes place, in fact; I will deny that I even know you but be very careful, the Zionist group are very crafty and they have tentacles spreading throughout the world."

"Thank you Klaus, I will not contact you until the deed has been done."

They both rose from their chairs and shook hands.

"Bill, do take care."

Bill Funk went straight home and his wife Bella had prepared a meal for him. When he had finished eating he retired to his study, he sat listening to his favourite music and pondering on his next move while drinking his brandy.

Having got the go ahead from Klaus he started to make a plan how he could achieve the revenge he had been thinking about for years.

Isaac Miller lived on the outskirts of Dusseldorf in a large house, which could be described as a mansion.

During the war it had been taken over by the Gestapo to be used as an interrogation centre, many government members who were opposed to Hitler's regime were brought to this building, tortured and in many cases murdered.

When Isaac was allowed back into his house he was sickened by the number of torturing instruments he found in the cellars and many other things that had been left behind when Germany capitulated and the occupants of the house fled to a neighbouring country rather than stand trial.

*

Count Jan Krupp called a meeting of his team to select the next person to be eliminated; he decided to backtrack and use the old castle on the outskirts Paris again.

Nathan and Peter travelled by ferry together, although they each had a government car they hired an older type car not their usual smart Jaguar vehicle they thought it might be safer as everyone is getting a little jumpy.

Arriving at the castle, they handed their car over to a security man who was on duty and they went into the main hall where hot and cold drinks were available.

Jan Krupp came out of a room inviting them all to join him, as they entered the room he greeted each one individually.

They all took their allocated seat and Jan related what had happened since their last meeting. He touched on the murder of Gordon and how this had taken place.

"I have been advised that Klaus Gunter has sent a team out in the field trying to identify the people who were responsible for the death of their comrades, fortunately he has been unsuccessful, as far as we know. It is a cat and mouse game at present."

"Right gentlemen, to the business on hand, I will deal the cards round, you all know the procedure by now."

The audible sighs of relief were heard as the cards were picked up;Peter looked across at Nathan and they both smiled and looked across the table, it was obvious by the look on Isaac Miller's face, he had picked up the Ace of Spades.

Jan picked up a small black bag.

"As you know gentlemen there are still six names in this bag."

He asked the gentleman seated third down the table to select a name from the bag.

The man pulled out a slip of paper and handed it to Jan.

"The name of the next person to receive our attention is Bill Funk.

This gentleman and his family organized groups of bully boys who went around smashing Jewish owned stores and shop windows. He also led the groups of bullies to wait outside the Synagogues waiting for families to emerge from their prayers and physically attack them, it didn't matter whether they were groups of men, women or children and they still beat them with truncheons or iron bars. Many still bear the scars of these attacks and some were maimed and of course many were transported to camps and they even cheered as the families were loaded on to railway cattle trucks to be transported to the concentration camps. It was not only Jewish families that were put on these trucks; it was any family or a member of a family who was considered a threat to the Nazi regime.

*

Isaac Miller had nurtured this hatred for many years that his family and friends should have been treated in this manner but now he has been given the opportunity to carry out his revenge but how he did not know. Isaac was sat drinking coffee at a pavement café bar reading a newspaper when a gentleman approached his table.

"May I join you?"

"Certainly, it is such a beautiful morning, how can I refuse company?"

"Thanks, you are Isaac Miller, yes?"

"Yes but we have not met before."

"My name is Bernie Black, you may have heard of me?"

"Indeed I have, why have you singled me out to join me for coffee?"

"My team has told me that you have been stalking Bill Funk, if you level with me I can help."

"From where have you got this information?"

"It doesn't matter but I am here to help you, I have a complete dossier on this man. Each evening after dinner he goes into his study to listen his favourite music.

After a while he starts drinking French Brandy, he still has a well stocked cellar of stolen French Brandy, he drinks heavily and in many cases he falls asleep in the study and stays there until the morning."

"We have hatched a plan to eliminate this vicious cowardly man, will you keep a low profile and leave us to deal with this man?"

"Yes, as you put it, I will keep a low profile for two weeks, if nothing has happened by that time I will become involved. Agreed?"

"Agreed"

*

Bill Funk and his wife decided to go away for a long week-end; his wife had been pressuring him to take some time off work to relieve the pressure he appears to be under.

Bernie and his team could not believe their good fortune, this gave Bernie an opportunity to enter Bill's house and it gave them the chance to decide what action to take. One of the team came up with an ingenious idea after visiting Bill's study. When he explained his idea to Bernie, he immediately said yes, go ahead and take the necessary steps to put your plan into operation.

Ten days later Isaac read in the newspaper that Bill Funk had died in his study. The report stated that he must have switched on the electric air-freshener and the by the time the container had warmed up enough to vaporize the contents of the small glass container, he was in a drunken sleep. The vapour entered the atmosphere of the room but instead of it being Bill's favourite Lavender aroma, it was a very potent nerve gas which killed Bill as he slept.

An investigation was carried out by the authorities, they checked the boxes in which the air-fresheners had been packed and delivered, they could not find any reason other than it was a mix up at the warehouse which caused an accidental death.

The coroner recorded it as an accidental death with no other person involved.

Isaac was just finishing his coffee when felt a tap on his shoulder.

"Care for another coffee?"

Isaac looked up and it was Bernie Black.

"Yes I will join you; we have something to talk about?"

"What is it you wish to discuss?"

"I just wanted to say, that I shall continue to keep a low profile."

They both burst out laughing.

"Isaac just you watch your back, it was you that Bill Funk had put in motion to eliminate, he blames you for all the chaos and financial loss his family suffered and the death of his grandfather when your family organized economic isolation of Germany in 1933."

He then contacted the Telegraph Newspaper to insert a notice reporting the sudden death of a member of the Smith family while on holiday in Brighton.

CHAPTER 7

A member of Klaus Gunter's team rang Klaus asking if he had read or had been told of the death reported in the Telegraph Newspaper, he replied, he had not read or heard of any deaths, in fact, he had not read any newspaper over the past few days as he had been quite ill. He then contacted Franz Sauckel and instructed him to investigate the newspaper report. Franz being one of his senior men, Klaus knew he would make a thorough search.

Two hours later Franz telephoned Klaus and told him that it was Bill Funk who had died or perhaps murdered and told Klaus the details.

Klaus was furious!

"Franz, go and collect the box of the remaining Air-fresheners and if possible get the one responsible for Bill's death. If you have any problem in obtaining these items, just tell them you are working for me that will open the door."

Franz went to the police station asking to speak to the police chief, he was shown into an office, after a minute or two a tall man with a military stature walked in.

"How can I help you sir?"

"Klaus Gunter has instructed me look into the death of Bill Funk."

"Yes, that was a very sad affair."

"He would like the remaining box of the air-fresheners and the bottle which caused his death.

If you are in any doubt, phone Klaus or your superior and I feel sure either one will give you the go ahead."

"I will go into my office and make a phone call"

I'll send you a cup of coffee to drink while you are waiting"

The police chief came back into the room accompanied by a constable who was carrying two boxes, one large and one small.

"These are the two boxes we took from Bill Funk's house when his death was being investigated. The boxes are numbered and I wish you to sign that you have taken the boxes from this station."

Franz signed the forms as requested and put the boxes into his car but before driving off he telephoned Klaus, he instructed Franz to deliver them to a certain address.

"Klaus, I have signed for these items, will you arrange for me to be given a receipt when I hand them over?"

*

Franz drove off to find the address Klaus had given him, after driving around the different streets in the area; he finally found the street he was looking for. He was very surprised to find such a broken down dirty looking building for a pharmaceutical business. He mounted the many steps leading to the main door, as he entered the building a uniformed gentleman approached him.

"Can I help you sir?"

"Yes I have these two parcels to deliver for Klaus Gunter."

"Come with me sir, you are expected."

Franz followed the doorman into a small room; they were followed by another man.

"Right Franz, it is Franz?"

"Yes, Klaus instructed me to deliver these two boxes to you but I must have a receipt."

"Here is the signed receipt and tell Officer Gunter I'll forward a report to him in two days time."

"Thank you; I'll bid you good day" and Franz left the building.

Franz was puzzled; he could not place the accent of the man he had been speaking to. He was convinced it was Korean or from that area, it could even have been Chinese. The name of the company on the building was written in Arabic, most unusual style for a German town.

*

Klaus called a meeting with the remaining team members.

"Gentlemen, again we have lost another comrade, Bill Funk. I have received a report from the pharmaceutical company who was engaged to look into the cause of Bill's death. The air-freshener that murdered Bill was the type that is inserted into an electric point and as it warms up, it vaporizes the contents and emits a pleasant odour into the atmosphere but the one which was plugged in had been tampered with and consequently it killed Bill. The seal had been had been broken, emptied and refilled with a toxic liquid. The forensic team is unable to identify the liquid or from where it came. I am convinced this murder was carried out by the vigilantes and his executioner was to be Isaac Miller. However, Isaac did not murder Bill, my informer was unsure who was responsible but it was a planned attack."

"The uncanny part of this unfortunate situation is when our last meeting was about to close, Bill asked to meet me in my office, do you remember?

Bill blamed Isaac Miller's family for organizing and attending rallies urging the world to boycott Germany economically in 1933. Bill's grandfather lost his business and his money and he committed suicide.

He also told me that he was going to take revenge on Isaac by killing him but the situation has gone in reverse, we must find out how this happened. I put it to you all; I think we ought to carry out Bill's mission.

Franz, you organize a complete dossier on Isaac and when you have a complete breakdown, I'll call another meeting and we will decide how we will act and when."

Franz organized a team of the top intelligence agents to carry out the surveillance and report back.

*

Colonel Black received a message from one of his team telling him that Isaac was being followed and his every movement is being watched.

Bernie Black went to the pavement café which he knew Isaac frequents several mornings each week; the third morning he found Isaac sat drinking coffee.

"Good morning, may I join you?"

Isaac looked up

"You most certainly can, what brings you to this part of the woods again?"

"You do! Klaus has had a team shadowing you for the past few days. He blames you for the death of Bill Funk and they intend to make you pay with your life."

"We must approach the situation very carefully and our first step will be to deal with your shadow and discover their intentions."

A gentleman approached their table.

"May I join you Bernie?"

"You most certainly can Walther but will it be safe for you to be seen speaking to me?"

"Walther, I owe you so much, you saved the life of my three year old great nephew when his parents were taken away."

"Since my daughter published the interview she carried out with me, I am constantly looking over my shoulder. I am often spoken to by people calling me Maurice, my old name."

"May I introduce you to Isaac Miller" Isaac stood up and shook hands.

"Bernie, it is Isaac I wanted to speak to you about. Klaus blames Isaac for Bill Funk's death and he has a team building up a dossier. When they have completed the dossier, a meeting is planned to decide how he will be eliminated. Isaac, I even know which cereal you had for your breakfast yesterday morning. What time you leave home in the mornings, where you get on and off the tram, from which paper vendor you collect your newspaper.

One thing they appear to be very interested in is the club you visit with your wife Tuesday and Thursday evenings".

"I would suggest, what you do is to change your daily routine, in fact, do the complete opposite every day to destroy their surveillance record up to date.

The team thinks that they have your movements completed but if you act as I say, you will throw a spanner in their works and it will become very interesting."

"Can we meet up one week today and I should be able to tell you if your change of routines had the effect we are looking for."

Isaac suddenly realized that he was in the firing line and he decided that he must alter his routine to stay alive.

Acting on Bernie Blacks suggestion, Isaac turned his daily routine upside down, every day he did the complete opposite to the previous day in every little detail hoping that this would fox the people who are trying to pin point his daily activities.

*

Klaus Gunter called a meeting with his team members. When they were all seated, he looked around saying.

"I have three dossiers relating to the daily routine of Isaac Miller, it is ridiculous, each dossier contradicts the findings of the others."

He sat staring round at the three agents who had been allocated the job of producing the dossiers.

His eyes were like pools of water with small pale blue pupils, the agents felt as he was staring at them, his eyes are similar to a laser beam boring into their brain and they found it most unnerving, many other people have experienced the same feeling in the past.

Klaus said, "I am not satisfied with our progress; I will engage a friend of mine, who, I feel sure will give us the answer how to approach the future."

He left the meeting feeling that he had been betrayed, his body jolted, Hans Joli will deal with this little problem, he is my man.

Arriving home, Klaus rang Hans.

"This is a voice from the past Hans, is it possible for us to meet, I have a little job I would like you to deal with for me?"

"I am not too sure I can undertake the little job, as you refer to but I will meet you and we can discuss it."

When Klaus and Hans met up in a coffee bar, Klaus related all that had taken place and how he had lost several of his friends.

"Hans, they were murdered, the last man to die was Bill Funk, you may remember him?"

"I remember him only too well."

"What I would like you to do, is to compile a complete dossier on Isaac Miller's daily movements, in fact, I am sure he was responsible for Bill Funks death. Three of my team completed a dossier on this man and each one contradicted the other, Miller must have been aware he was being followed. He might think he is clever but we will nail him eventually."

"I am relying on you to come up with a spot- on dossier, I will be most grateful if you will deal with problem for me."

Klaus got out of his chair, shook hands with Hans and walked off, Hans remained seated and his mind drifted back to the last job given to him by Klaus.

*

Klaus instructed him to visit a French village during the wartime occupation as they were confident that a resistance group was operating from there. Hans and his senior Officer Bill Funk went to the village accompanied with a truck containing 10 troopers and they were going to interrogate the villagers about the local resistance group members but not one of the villagers knew, or would admit to knowing the men or women involved.

They made no progress, Bill Funk instructed his troopers to march the women and children into the village church and one small boy watched his mother and small sister go into the church, he was hiding and he could do nothing. They continued questioning, pressing their attention on the children but they did not gain any information.

Funk came out of the church and instructed his men to lock all the doors leading in or out of the church, when they were all secure, they sprayed the doors with petrol and set fire to the building. Hans still hears the screams in his nightmares. Hans got into Funks car and as they drove off, there was a terrific explosion, the troop carrier and the 10 soldiers were in small pieces. Hans did not agree with Funks action but he would have been regarded as a weakling if he had tried to dissuade his senior officer from taking the action he had taken.

Hans shook himself, he had been thinking back over the events of a few years ago, he thought to himself that Bill Funk deserved a more painful death than just dying in a drunken sleep, perhaps he will suffer burning in hell.

He was not blamed for the incineration of the villagers; it was recorded as being the result of a powerful explosion which not only killed the soldiers but it destroyed part of the church and set it on fire and the occupants were unable to get out due to the piles of bricks and glass.

The resistance people were blamed but Hans knew differently, Bill Funk was to blame.

When Han arrived home he discussed Klaus's request with his wife, she agreed that he should go ahead with the report but on completion, hand it over and take no further part in whatever Klaus is planning.

"We are too old to get involved with all this espionage business and we now have a lovely family life with our daughters and grandchildren, Hans please keep it that way."

*

The following morning Hans left home armed with a tape recorder and a camera hoping to create a dossier on Isaac Miller for Klaus. He was a little disturbed the way Klaus had referred to Isaac in such a manner that it means Isaac is in danger.

Hans followed Isaac's movements for two days, the second day was totally different from the first and he could understand why Klaus's team got it wrong. The third morning, as he left his house, a large car pulled up alongside him and two burly men got out of the car and bundled him into the back seat of the car. He was taken to a small office where Walther and Bernie were waiting for him.

"Why are you shadowing Isaac Miller?"

Bernie took the tape recorder and his camera from Hans's shoulder bag,

"It is useless denying it, you too have been followed."

"Hans, for whom are you collecting this information, is it Klaus?"

"Yes, Klaus asked me to compile a dossier on Isaac's movements, for what reason I don't know."

Bernie turned to him saying.

"He blames Isaac Miller for the death of Bill Funk but it was not he that was responsible, you may pass this information on if you wish. Funk was not as blameless as he pretended to be.

I have some intelligence reports on his activities during the German occupation of France. You know what I am saying is correct, I know that you were present at one of his atrocities; the true happenings were never made public. He did not deserve to live."

"Klaus asked me to complete this dossier that is all; I have given my wife my word that I will not get involved any further.

We are enjoying a good life with our family and grandchildren; I have no intention of disrupting our life style."

"I am pleased hear you say that Hans, we will give you a completed dossier for you to hand in, would that satisfy you?"

"Yes, that will be ideal."

"My boys will take you home."

They shook hands and Hans left the room.

*

Several days later Hans found an envelope on the mat in the hall at his home.

Hans opened the envelope, the first thing he saw was a note signed by Bernie, expressing a wish that this dossier will meet his requirements.

Reading the papers, they certainly agreed with Isaacs's daily routine for the past seven days, there was one clever twist, on the third and the sixth day he altered his routine.

I feel sure that Klaus will accept this report, however, if Isaac should change his pattern of behaviour, Han's could not be held responsible, this report relates to the past seven days.

Hans telephoned Klaus and arranged a meeting, when they did meet up Hans handed him the report to read.

When he finished reading the dossier, he looked up.

"Hans, this is excellent, I am most grateful. Cheers for now and take good care of yourself and your family."

"Klaus, having compiled this for you, I do not want anymore to do with whatever your plans are."

"O K. Hans, you did what I asked you and I am most grateful, I will ask no more of you.

CHAPTER 8

Colonel Black made a point of visiting Isaac Millers favourite coffee bar and he saw Isaac sitting at a table alone.

"Hello Isaac, are you well and relaxed?"

"Yes but I am still looking over my shoulder bearing in mind what you told me."

"Klaus has accepted the dossier laying out your movements, which was compiled by my team."

"Two evenings ago I spoke to your uncle, Ben Solomon and as you know he now lives in America. We discussed your situation and he would like you and your family to visit him in America and stay with him for a while. He will engage a reliable man to maintain the running of your business exporting and importing mobile phones, cameras and various electrical components."

"I want your wife and two young sons to be seen leaving the house by taxi bound for the airport, you wave them off and then walk back into your house. It would appear that you are staying at home alone but I want you to walk out of the back door where a car will be waiting for you, your suitcase will have been loaded into the car earlier. Your family will board a schedule flight to America but you will be taken a small airport where you will board a private Jet belonging to your uncle.

I have a man who is the same stature as yourself, his hair has been styled as yours and will wear your clothes and in fact they will be convinced that it is you in the house by yourself."

If any of Klaus's team should visit your house we will be ready for him. I will contact you when all the plans have been put in place, obviously I expect you to discuss it with your wife but not your boys, they might let it slip out to one of their friends and that would jeopardize the whole plan and that would make it dangerous."

*

Arriving home he received his usual welcome, kissed by his wife and hugged by his boys, they all sat down at the table as a family to enjoy dinner prepared by their mother Sadie, she could see that Isaac had a problem on his mind. When the meal was finished, the boys went upstairs to finish their homework or listen to their music. Sadie turned to Isaac.

"What is bothering, you have something on your mind?"

"I will tell you but what I am going to say is strictly confidential, you must not mention a word of it to anyone, especially the boys.

Uncle Ben is arranging for us to go and spend some time with him in America"

"What for Isaac?"

"Many years ago my grandparents and their families organized rallies throughout the world calling for the world to boycott Germany economically in 1933 and it crippled Germany, causing chaos and because of that I was going to be killed by Bill Funk but he was found dead in his study, for which I have been blamed.

Bill Funk said my family was responsible for his granddad losing his vast import and export business, his money and his grandfather committed suicide."

*

Bernie contacted Isaac giving him the date and time for their departure to America was planned to take place. Sadie had secretly packed two suit cases for her and the boys, Isaac's case had been packed earlier and left by the back door.

The evening before the plan was going to be put into operation; they sat at the table for a meal and one of Bernie's team sat down with them. Sadie remarked how much the man named Mark looked like her husband Isaac, especially when he slipped into one of Isaac's outfit. The two boys were mystified and asked their mother, what is going on?

Sadie sat them down and explained the situation regarding their father to them.

"Why didn't you tell us before now?"

"It is a complete secret and we were afraid you might let it slip, had you done so your father would be in great danger. I must emphasize that you must not telephone any of your friends telling them that you are off to America, otherwise all the preparation will have been to no avail. I must ask you both to promise me that you will not contact a soul; otherwise the death of your father will be on your conscience for the rest of your lives.

We have not told my parents or the Rabbi. You can telephone your friends from America but you must not mention that your father is with us.

Doing it this way the people who have put a contract on your father will think he is here alone but it will be Mark."

The boys got very excited.

"Do you know who is trying to kill our father?"

"No we do not know who is responsible but we know it could happen if we are not very careful."

*

The following morning they all sat down to enjoy breakfast, Isaac was fully dressed but he was wearing a robe over his clothing, Mark was wearing Isaac's shirt and trousers.

Ten o'clock a taxi came to a halt at the front door, Isaac still wearing the bathrobe carried out the suitcases and it was a tearful farewell, most convincing, he waited to wave them off until the car turned the street corner.

He went back into the house, when he was away from the window he removed the robe and handed it to Mark who then put it on over his clothing.

Isaac went out of the back door and was delighted to see a car waiting for him, the driver had collected his case from inside the back door and put it in the car. The driver turned round to speak to Isaac.

"Bernie told me to take an indirect route to the small airfield, just to ensure we are not being followed."

Forty minutes later the driver pointed to a small airstrip and they could see a twin jet engine plane was waiting on the runway. The driver took the car alongside the plane; a man was standing on the steps, he jumped down and shook Isaac by the hand and then he took the suitcase from the driver. The driver waved cheerio to Isaac and drove off.

The driver stopped the car and watched the plane getting airborne. The small plane will land in Amsterdam and then Isaac will catch a scheduled flight which will mean the family will arrive at JFK several hours before their father.

*

As Isaac and his family left their home, Bernie's team went into the house and proceeded to install small cameras to cover each room. The cameras would record any activity to the receiver in the small white van parked further down the street.

Mark left the house well wrapped up in an overcoat and scarf with his coat collar turned up. The family car was not required for the school run so he drove himself as if to work.

Two hours after him leaving the house, two men each dressed as workmen carrying a small tool box entered Isaac's house, all their activity was being watched and recorded as they went from room to room.

The two men appeared to be interested in household electrical system and they ran a cable from a wall plug to a point under the sink in the kitchen. Although the people in the van could identify where they were working but couldn't pinpoint the exact position to where the cable is attached.

They left the house one hour later, as they were walking away they were laughing and joking looking very pleased with themselves, they were convinced they had carried out to Klaus's instruction to the letter.

The technical team in the van telephoned Colonel Black; he caught a taxi to two streets from the van and walked. When he viewed the recordings and studied what work that had been carried out, he immediately contacted his electrical technicians as it was obvious that an electrical booby trap had been set.

Two of Bernie's electrician's entered Isaac's house through the rear door hoping that the house was not under surveillance at this time of the day. They found the taps had been made live and would surely electrocute any person turning on the taps.

They set to work and removed the cable that had been taken under the floor boards which is connected to the taps.

It is obvious that Klaus expects a result.

Bernie decided to gamble, he instructed the electrician to make the house safe for Mark.

"I want the kitchen lights on and Mark to be seen using the taps without causing him any injury and I feel sure the intruders will return tomorrow to investigate why the booby trap did not work."

One of the electricians remained in the house and at the crack of dawn he bypassed the main switch box, should the intruder return to check their booby trap and switch off the mains, the plugs would still remain live.

Bernie's gamble paid off, the two intruders entered Isaac's house using the house keys and one of them turned off the main electrical supply and the other took a spanner from his bag and went to remove a tap, as his spanner came in contact with the tap there was a blue flash and the man was thrown to the floor, his pal tried to resuscitate him but unsuccessfully and he realised his heart had stopped, we have been had. He dragged his pal outside and made a phone call asking for assistance, several minutes later a van pulled up, a man jumped down from the van and proceeded to examine the injured electrician with his stethoscope, after checking he looked up and shook his head.

When he arrived back at Klaus's office, the electrician was trembling, not only did Klaus shout at him, he physically attacked him, shouting he was an incompetent electrician.

The man who had remained hidden in the house contacted Bernie giving him the full details. Bernie smiled, he thought, job well done. He told the man to ensure the electrical system in the house was now made completely safe.

Another message which made him sit up was that Klaus is under pressure from a powerful body threatening to replace him if he doesn't sort out the constant vigilante activity.

*

When the aircraft carrying Sadie and the boys landed at JFK, she was delighted to find Uncle Ben there to meet them, he was very impressed with the boys. He took them to the restaurant for a light meal and a drink.

The boys were having difficulty in keeping their excitement under control. Ben gave the boys some money to play on the fruit machines that were not restricted by age.

This gave him time to speak to Sadie and he told her what had taken place after they left their house.

"I do hope Mark was not injured?"

"No Bernie dealt with the whole plan beautifully."

"Right, I have a car waiting outside to take you to our house. Auntie Sophie is so excited to have you as our guests, you will have to make allowances if she tends to spoil the boys, as you may know we lost our boy when he was eight years of age and she has never got over the loss.

His birth was a difficult one and she was unable to have any more children.

Ben's chauffeur had loaded the luggage on the car and they set off. They were driving for about forty five minutes when Ben pointed to a large house beyond several paddocks fenced off with white five bar gates with several horses grazing; as they approached the house the boys were so excited.

"Are they your horse's Uncle Ben?"

"Yes, do you ride?"

"We have never tried."

"In that case, I will get Nat to teach you."

Sophie was on the doorstep, she was so excited, so much so she was in tears and Ben had been right, it was the two boys she was interested in. She turned to Ben.

"I have a message."

"Isaac's plane is due in three hours time."

"Harry, will you meet Isaac's plane please, you will need to display a notice otherwise he will not know who is meeting him."

*

Klaus called a meeting with the members of his team and he had great difficulty in controlling his temper as he related what had taken place with the planned elimination of Isaac. He had instructed several of his security people to be present at the meeting and listen to his ranting on how,

The Master Race has been outwitted by a Jew; I will take steps to ensure we are in control once more.

The meeting was about to be brought to a close, Klaus was called to take a phone call.

When he picked up the phone, a man's voice at the other end of the line said.

"Meet me in The Regent Berlin Hotel next Thursday morning at eleven o'clock, no ifs or buts, just you be there." Klaus was taken aback; he was not used to be spoken like that but realized by the tone of the man's voice he had to attend.

CHAPTER 9

Klaus was feared by his own team and his enemies alike but the tone of the man's voice on the telephone made him a little nervous of what to expect on Thursday morning and from whom.

Klaus arranged for his car to be available to take him to Berlin on Thursday morning. As he arrived at the hotel, a young man came down the steps to meet him.

"Are you Mr. Klaus Gunter sir?"

"Yes I am."

"Kindly follow me."

The young man guided him through the foyer into a room where coffee had been made available.

"Please make yourself comfortable sir and I will take you to the reserved room when I am called."

He sat with a cup of coffee and smoking a cigarette wondering why he had been called.

Ten minutes later the door opened and the young man indicated for him to follow. They went into the lift, pushed the button to go to the seventh floor. Stepping out of the lift, Klaus walked along a long corridor and taken to a door, he knocked on the door and a gruff voice bid him to enter.

Klaus entered the hotel room, he was met by two men with a military bearing , both about six feet six inches tall, wide shoulders and heavily built. He stepped forward to introduce himself offering his hand, the man took a step back, clicked his heels and raised his arm giving the Nazi salute and the second man did the same.

Klaus recognized them; they were, Frank von Kessler and Fritz Beckenbaugh both very prominent influential business men. Kessler was wearing a black eye patch covering his right eye, which gave him an evil aura. Klaus was invited to sit down.

All three sat down in comfortable easy chairs.

Frank looked at Klaus.

"Our wonderful Fuehrer would be devastated by the number of errors made by one of his Senior Generals over the past few years. You have never been short of money to carry out your duties, in fact; perhaps too much money has been drafted in your direction. You were selected to chair the meeting in Dusseldorf in1939 and the minutes of the meeting eventually ended up in an old cinema in the City of Liverpool in England, how could that be?

The old cinema was selected and fitted out in readiness for when we invaded Britain, you were instructed to acquire the building but you failed, not only did you fail but in the process two of our senior officers ended up in prison.

Klaus, we still intend to control Europe as one country with Germany completely in charge, as our Fuehrer intended.

We failed to achieve our objective because of people like you, who was incapable of carrying out their duties in spite of our superior strength?"

"I understand that you made an attempt to eliminate Isaac Miller and yet again you failed, why? This man was responsible for the death of Bill Funk, why then is Miller still alive?"

Klaus was not used to being bombarded with questions; it is he who normally asks the questions.

"A complete dossier was compiled of his daily routine but for some reason the dossier did not prove to be correct and Miller escaped our trap."

"Klaus Gunter, Miller is now in America staying with his uncle, Ben Solomon, this man escaped the authorities in Germany during 1938. He was assisted by two German friends who paid the price with their lives, they faced a firing squad. I have all the necessary details of where to find him, this will give you another opportunity to eliminate him.

If we find you are no longer capable making the right decisions and acting on them, you will be replaced.

We will be watching your progress very carefully but remember, we will no longer tolerate failure."

Klaus left the hotel feeling very annoyed having received such treatment from a civilian and he being such a senior officer in the German Army.

*

Isaac and his family were soon settled and the boys were really enjoying being spoiled by their Auntie Sophie. Several days after their arrival, Nat collected Simon and Luke and took them a room above the stables where he kitted them out with riding gear. When they went back to the house and entered the room, Ben jumped to his feet.

"Simon, leave that whip here, no one, I repeat no one uses a whip on my horses, I will not allow a jockey to use a whip on any horse belonging to me, even in a race."

"What horses are you going to put the boys on Nat?"

"I thought the two docile mares, Mandy and Mary."

"A very good choice but you must be very careful if you take the Black Stallion, he is very volatile at times."

Nat took the boys to the stables; he showed them how to saddle the horses, both mares stood perfectly still as he demonstrated placing the bit in the mouth and how to adjust the straps to hold the saddle securely. He gave both boys a lift into the saddle and ensured that their feet were correctly in the stirrups.

They set off just walking the horses, Nat watched them very carefully, Luke appeared to adapt easier than Simon. They jogged around the perimeter of the fenced paddock and the boys thoroughly enjoyed the ride, it was an experience for them.

When they arrived back at the stables, they were given a lesson on how to remove the saddle and bridle. The next lesson was how to brush the horses down and put them in their stable and feed them some oats.

The boys dashed back to the house, they were so excited.

Ben looked up from his paper.

"Well, how did you get on, did you enjoy yourselves?"

"It was wicked Uncle Ben, can we ride tomorrow?"

"I don't see any reason why not."

Sophie came into the room with two bowls of ice-cream and handed them to the boys, Sadie smiled.

"Uncle Ben?"

"Yes Simon"

"When we were cantering round the fence perimeter near the wooded area, I saw two men with binoculars watching this house, who are they?"

Ben looked straight at Isaac.

"I have two horses entered into races next week and they are both long odds, they were possibly timing the horses while they were training. That is the only explanation I can think of."

*

Ben tried to contact Colonel Black the following morning but was unsuccessful; he left his name and number saying he would like to speak to him.

Later that evening Bernie telephoned Ben.

Ben explained about the two men who had been spotted in the woodland area watching the house with binoculars.

"I told the boys who spotted them that they would be punters spying on my horses and timing their training gallops but we both know differently."

"Right Ben, I will send a man to visit you tomorrow, show him around the stables, if you are being watched it will appear he is interested in nothing but the horses. Indicate the area where the two men were seen and his team will look into the reason why they are there.

While we are speaking Ben, Isaac did not kill Bill Funk, it was a young Frenchman who saw his mother and sister marched into a church which Bill Funk had all the doors locked and set fire to the building and the fifteen women, children and a priest perished in the fire during the German occupation of France. The boy was five years of age and he has carried that hate in his heart for all these years.

He had waited all these years and he jumped at the chance to be the one to empty the liquid from air-freshener and refill it with the toxic substance which killed Bill Funk.

Sadly, Jacques was killed in a car accident on the German Autobahn as he was driving back to France.

In spite of an enquiry into the car accident, no definite conclusion was reached. I intend to send the report of who killed Bill Funk and the newspaper report of the accidental death of Bill Funk's assassin to Klaus; it will be arranged for him to receive it secretly.

After dinner Ben and Isaac went out for a stroll and Ben was able to tell Isaac about his conversation with Bernie.

*

Lunchtime the following day, a white van arrived at the house, painted on the sides of the van in large writing, read, "Specialists in Grass for Race Tracks." They reported to the house and Ben gave them the go ahead to check his training tracks, it was obvious they had been sent by Bernie.

The four men who came with the van walked along the tracks probing the ground and examining the soil. They paid particular attention to the sharp turn by the woods, while they were busy checking, the fourth man went into the wooded area to carry out a search. After a while, the man came out carrying a small polythene bag, in the bag were several cigarette and cigar stubs. Two hours was spent by the men and they reported to Ben, saying they were leaving.

"Before we leave Mr. Solomon, the wooded area by the sharp turn, is it you property?"

"Yes it is"

"So anybody in that area would be trespassing?"

"Yes they would be."

The four men got into the van and drove off; they went straight to their office and telephoned Colonel Black. He instructed that the wooded area should be kept under constant surveillance.

"Do not try arrest any one for trespassing, just make sure you get good photographs, we will then know what, or who we are dealing with but do make sure one of the photographs will show both men's full face and fax me copies, Okay?"

Chapter 10

Bernie was sitting at a pavement café bar enjoying the sunshine, his coffee and smoking a cigar, he was pondering how he could find the time to take his wife away on a short holiday.

His wife Lottie was giving him a hard time because he is spending so little time at home these days and he too felt he would enjoy a break from the constant pressure. He was sat trying to find the answer when a tap on his shoulder brought him back to earth, a waiter handed him a slip of paper saying.

"Telephone this gentleman when you return to your office and treat it as very urgent. That is the phone message I have just taken"

"Thank you Karl."

Bernie drank his coffee, left money on the table to cover the cost of his bill and returned to his office and rang the telephone number shown on the slip of paper. It was ringing out and Bernie heard the phone being picked up and a man's voice spoke saying,

"This is the FBI Department and Jim Code speaking."

"This is Colonel Black, you asked me to call."

"Good lord Bernie it is a long time since we last met or even spoke. I will tell you why it is I have contacted you.

We intercepted the photographs your agent has faxed you and we would like to put you in the picture. The two men have been under surveillance by the FBI for some considerable time as we suspect them to be the brains behind the kidnapping gang, not the people chasing Isaac Miller."

"How do you know about Isaac?"

"It is our job to know everything that is going on in this country. We are convinced this group is guilty of kidnapping the children of wealthy parents and grandparents but we do not have enough evidence to arrest and deport the ringleader. Over the past year they have carried out several kidnappings, the second kidnapping was tragic, the parents were unable raise the money and the grandparents would not or could not help and the little boy was found drowned, face down in the next door neighbour's swimming pool.

From that day the parents did not contact the police or refuse to pay the ransom money for the return of their child. The FBI is convinced that the ransom money is being siphoned off to a Neo Nazi group, which is becoming very active in the U.S.A.

*

The reason Ben Solomon is being watched, Isaac's two boys are staying with him, we think Ben is the target. Ben is very wealthy and he left Germany in 1938, just before he and his family were due to be taken to a labour camp and a family member of a senior officer of the Nazi Party was going to take his money, property and his business but Ben and his family escaped with their money, which, he had very carefully managed to transfer to this country. He had been warned by his German friends who were shot for helping Ben, he has never been forgiven for cheating the master race that is still how they refer to themselves.

This gang intends to get a lot of ransom money from Ben for the release of the two boys, who, they are planning to kidnap.

We would like you to come to USA to help us get to grips with the situation, it is said that you have agents everywhere and your team can cope with any situation?"

"I doubt if my boss will allow me to fly and stay in America."

"Bernie, you will receive a phone call instructing you to come here shortly, Senator Clive Reeves telephoned your boss to make this request and your boss agreed."

Bernie was mystified by the happenings; he leaned over the desk to replace the receiver on the pod. As he sat up the phone began to ring, he picked up the phone.

"Hello, this is Colonel Black"

"Hello Bernie, I would like you to undertake an assignment in the USA as something appears to be brewing, take your wife with you and make it look like a holiday visit. Senator Clive Reeves will arrange for you to be met at the airport and taken to your hotel, nothing will be left to chance."

"Certainly sir but what is happening?"

"Colonel Black, the Senator will give you the full details of what is happening at Ben Solomon's Ranch and you are to organize your team to prevent an incident."

"I will plan to leave in two days time, this will give me time to clear my desk and give my wife time to make necessary arrangement cancelling papers etc."

"Right Bernie, I will leave it with you."

*

Arriving home Lottie had his meal ready for him, as he sat at the table eating his meal he turned to his wife.

"You said it is time we had a holiday, could you be packed and ready to go in two days time?"

"I am so bothered about your health, I can be packed and ready for the off in a few hours. Where are you planning to take me?"

"America, Senator Reeves is arranging everything for us; we are being met at the airport and taken to a hotel which has been booked for us."

"I hope it is a holiday and not just another assignment."

"It is a little of both, I have to just set plans in motion then it will be up to my team leader to take it from there."

They sat looking at each other,

"Bernie I am so pleased to be going away and we can spend some time together."

As he left the table the phone began to ring, he picked the phone up.

"Hello, this is Colonel Black."

"Hi! Bernie, this Ben Solomon, the men are watching this house again, have you any idea what is going on?"

"Yes, the FBI is of the opinion that it is a kidnapping gang who are concentrating on the two boys, not Isaac. I have been instructed to fly to your area; I shall be with you in a couple of days. It is of the utmost importance that you do not let Luke and his brother Simon out of your sight. I will put you in the complete picture when I arrive."

"Bernie, why don't you and Lottie stay here, we have plenty of room?"

"That is very kind of your offer but Senator Reeves is making all the arrangements but I will bear your offer in mind. I feel sure that Lottie would be more comfortable with you rather than a hotel."

*

The following morning the postman delivered a long business looking envelope addressed to Mr. and Mrs. Black, Lottie pulled out the small envelope from the inside of the larger envelope and she excitedly saw two first class plane tickets to America.

Arriving home Bernie could see that Lottie was excited and she showed him the tickets and she was jumping about like a young child. Needless to say she had very little sleep that night, they were up very early and the car to take them to the airport came to a halt outside their house at eight o'clock.

They passed through the check in desk fairly quickly, the security took the longer which was understandable, their bags and their person was checked.

When the plane was airborne Bernie ordered a bottle of wine hoping this would calm Lottie down, it did and she was asleep after the second glass of the wine. Bernie went to sleep and it was the captain's voice wakened him saying they would be landing in thirty minutes time.

They got off the plane and when they went the carousel to collect their luggage, again they were checked and asked why have they come to the US, Holiday or Business.

Finally they got through all the final checks and interviews, a man with a peaked cap stood holding a board with their name written on it.

Lottie and Bernie made their way through the crowds to the gentleman.

"Hi! My name Mr. Black and this is my wife."

"Good, let me take your luggage Mrs. Black," he took her cases and carried them out to the car and placed them in the boot of the car.

The car looked a cumbersome ugly looking vehicle, similar to the type a farmer would use.

Lottie and Bernie sat in the rear seats of the car and remarked how comfortable the seats were.

"Mr. Black, if you pull the flap down the back of the seat in front of you, you will find a thermos flask of coffee or there is a selection of drinks."

"Thank you, what is your name?"

"Gary sir"

"Thank you Gary, how far is it to the hotel that has been booked for us?"

"The journey will take approximately one hour."

They relaxed on the seat holding hands enjoying the trip and looking at the landscape and the hills, they were away from all the built up areas, beautiful countryside.

*

Thirty minutes into their journey Gary said.

"We are being followed, it might one of our people and I do hope so."

The large black limousine pulled out of the traffic lane and came alongside their car and started firing hand guns at the rear passenger seats.

"My god Gary, what is going on?"

"I don't know but do not worry this vehicle is armour plated and has bullet proof windows and tyres. I will call Senator Reeves."

"We are being attacked sir, he described the attacking car and they are attempting to push us off the road."

"Gary switch on the identification light on the car roof, a helicopter will be with you in two minutes."

Bernie could see the helicopter coming over the hilltop. The helicopter could not attack as the two cars were too close; the attacking car was still trying to push them off the road.

A voice came over the intercom.

"Gary, when I give you the word, brake suddenly, this will give me a clear shot at your assailant."

Gary waited until the car came along side attempting to push them off the road and the man in the helicopter shouted "Now" Gary braked hard the other car carried on, Bernie heard the pop of small cannon fire, the black car swerved and burst into flames and rolled down the embankment and it exploded when it reached the bottom.

Lottie turned to Bernie.

"What the hell have you brought me here for? I was looking forward to a restful holiday together but it hasn't started that way. That could have been us that rolled down the embankment on fire."

Senator's voice came over the car phone, "Everything okay, Gary?"

"Yes thank you sir, the helicopter certainly put paid to the gunmen."

"Bernie, did you tell anyone you were visiting this country for any reason?"

"No, perhaps Lottie mentioned it when she cancelled the papers; she is shaking her head saying no. Just one moment, Ben phoned last night and I told him not to let Luke or Simon out of his sight and I also told him that I would be joining him in a day or two but I feel sure Ben would not repeat it."

*

Arriving at the hotel, two gentlemen both looking like Man Mountain came down the steps to greet them, they picked up the luggage and asked Bernie and Lottie to follow them. Bernie started to walk towards the reception desk but he was just waved away, one of the men had their allocated room keys.

Gary turned to Bernie.

"These two gentlemen will be staying in the hotel to keep an eye on you and to ensure your safety."

When they got into their room and by themselves, Lottie thumped Bernie's shoulder.

"Tell me what you are up to, why all the secrecy and don't you dare tell me a cock and bull story, there is something going on. If you don't tell me the truth, I am not unpacking my bags and I am going straight back home, I am not endangering my life for nothing?"

"Lottie, switch the radio on loudly and let us go into the bathroom, it is unlikely any listening device will be in the bathroom.

It appears that an organized kidnapping group is in operation in this country concentrating on the very rich. The one we are going to meet is Ben Solomon; he left Germany in 1938 much to the annoyance of the Nazi Party.

They intend to kidnap Isaac's two boys Luke and Simon and the ransom will be a substantial sum. The ransom money is said to be passed to a Neo Nazi group which, is gaining ground in this country, the FBI is becoming very concerned about this movement.

"Thank you Bernie, I now know we can expect anything to happen during our restful holiday together."

"Don't be sarcastic Lottie, I have told you exactly as things are and I for one did not expect the car incident, it is not as if I am a senator but we were in one of his security armoured cars."

"Lottie smiled; she leaned forward and kissed Bernie on his cheek."

Bernie secretly smiled to himself, job done.

Chapter 11

They both got showered and changed their clothing to go down for dinner. "Have you the key Bernie?" Asked Lottie as they left the room, they went into the lift which would take them straight into the restaurant.

As they walked to the desk, the Maitre D! Guided them to a table in the corner of the room away from the window and their two minders were sitting on the next table between them and the door. Bernie smiled; the move is exactly as shown in the security manual.

The people in the restaurant looked at them with suspicion wondering who they were and why they were surrounded with security.

Lottie enjoyed the waiter being so attentive and she thoroughly enjoyed her meal and she also thought the wine suggested by the waiter was delicious.

They decided to have their coffee served in the lounge and Bernie enjoyed a cognac with his coffee and his usual cigar.

Lottie suggested they stay in the lounge for a while and have another drink before going up to their room and after a while they went to their room and watched the TV for a while before going to bed. When they did go to bed they found it so comfortable, they were soon asleep and slept until the alarm clock woke them at eight o'clock.

*

The following morning they went down to the breakfast room and found it to be very busy but a waiter took them to the same table as the night before.

Having finished his breakfast, Bernie went across to the two security men.

"I would like to go to Ben Solomon's ranch this morning, is it okay if I get the desk to call me a cab?"

"Come down when you are ready and we will arrange transport for you"

Lottie said, "Come along Bernie" he followed her to the lift.

Back in their room, Lottie went to the bathroom and while she was there Bernie changed his jacket for a lighter and a loose fitting one this allowed him to wear his shoulder holster without it being obvious that he was carrying the gun that had been given to him by one of the security men.

As they entered the foyer, one of the men went outside to look around and then he beckoned Bernie to follow. The vehicle was a smaller version of the car they travelled in the day before. One of the men sat in the front with the driver.

"Are you comfortable in the back sir?"

"Yes thank you, we are very comfortable."

They drove off, they were travelling for forty minutes when they came to a large field surrounded with white fencing and there were ten horses grazing in the field, which, later Bernie was told to refer to as a paddock.

The driver took the car down a long driveway to the ranch; Ben was standing on the veranda to welcome them and he took Bernie and Lottie into the house and all the introductions took place.

Sophia and Lottie did not need to be introduced; they had been close friends many years earlier. When all the introductions were over, the security man said he would stay until they went back to the hotel. Sophia was so excited to see Lottie she then tried to persuade her to get Bernie to agree to move from the hotel to the ranch.

*

Ben, Isaac and Bernie went into another room leaving the women to themselves.

"Ben, have you explained the details I told you over the phone?"

"Yes Bernie but we are a little hesitant about telling the ladies, they would panic."

"I am going to tell you two gentlemen, I don't know what is happening, yesterday Lottie and I were travelling from the airport to the hotel and a car came alongside and we were attacked by gunfire and the car tried to put us off the road into a ravine.

The reason we were safe was the vehicle was armour plated and the tyres and windows were bullet proof."

Ben started laughing, "Let's have a drink, the ugly people always get attacked in this country and you qualify Bernie", they all started to laugh.

"Your two German friends who helped you were shot for helping you to transfer your money and escape."

"Yes I was very sad that should happen, both families have been here and I have been fortunate enough to help them set up a business in this country. Also, their sons went to the best college in the USA, it was the least I could do."

Have you a horse that would carry Man Mountain who is to stay with us until we go back to the hotel, can we go out riding in a group?"

"Certainly, we can go on the back paddock road and double back in a circle on to the perimeter to where we should surprise the watchers."

"Do you mean a group including the boys?"

"Yes, let us push them into taking some sort of action."

Ben left Bernie alone, he and Isaac went back to join the ladies, which, gave Bernie the opportunity to telephone his team in the hopes of coming up with some plan to de-fuse the situation.

Bernie and his wife Lottie were preparing to return to their hotel, Sophia said.

"Hang on Bernie, the phone is ringing."

After a short while Ben came back into the room.

"Can you come to lunch tomorrow, Senator Reeves intends to join us and he will put you in the picture of all that is happening?"

"I don't see why not." Looking at the security men, one of them nodded.

"Yes Ben, at what time?"

"Lunch at 12.30 is that okay with you?"

"Yes that will be okay?"

Sophia turned to Lottie. "Check out of the hotel and stay here with us, we would be delighted to have your company."

"I think it would be a good idea, we will be on the spot." Both Sophia and Lottie looked at Bernie.

Bernie suddenly realized he had said the wrong thing, however, the next morning they did check out of the hotel and planned to stay with Sophia and Ben on their ranch. Lottie smiled to herself, Sophia and she had planned this to happen.

The security men can have the spare chauffeurs flat, which, is quite luxurious.

When they returned to the ranch the following day, they found that the Senator was there accompanied with his wife Hilda. After all the introductions had taken place the party was taken for a tour round the stables. One of the stable girls was walking a beautiful brown filly round a circuit between two rows of stables. The horses coat shone in the sunshine and the hoofs had been painted with varnish or some such liquid to make them shine also, it looked a complete picture of health.

The Senator was walking round the animal.

"What a wonderful looking horse."

"Yes, Tilley is running in the Gold Cup next week."

"Will she win?"

"Sometimes in her training gallops, she clocks very good times but during a race she likes to run behind another horse. We are trying to break her habit."

"Uncle Ben, can we go to the races next week?"

"I am not too sure about that Simon; we will have to talk about it."

*

They all went back into the house, Lottie and Sophia had prepared the lunch and it was a complete success.

When the meal was over they decided to take their coffee in the lounge but Ben looked at the Senator.

"Shall we take our coffee in the other room, then, you can talk to Bernie." Ben picked up a pot of coffee and Harry Reeves, Isaac and Bernie followed him.

The Senator turned to Bernie.

"Tell us your story," he said smiling.

"My team has pinpointed the exact spot the watchers stand while using their binoculars, we have installed the very latest in the camera technology, they are only as thick as a pencil and two inches long, they can be zoomed to get close up pictures or freeze on one frame to obtain a still picture. They also pick up speech which can be amplified to give as loud as you wish. The three cameras are taped to a bough of a tree, very difficult to see from the ground, they are controlled by the technology installed in a small van about ½ a mile away."

The Senator turned to Bernie.

"Are they really as good as the picture you have painted?"

"I have brought a DVD disk with me to give you a demonstration."

Bernie walked over to the TV and inserted the disk in the DVD player.

At first it just displayed the undergrowth of woodland; it then showed two men standing near a hedgerow. A voice over, told them the man was going to pull a page from a newspaper and you can see how the camera increases its magnification to pick up the writing. He held up the paper and print on the paper gradually increased in size until you could read the words on the screen. The man is speaking but you cannot hear but the volume is going to be increased and the man's voice got louder and eventually it sounded as if he was standing next to them.

"Bernie, I am very impressed, it is ingenious."

"Now you witnessed this demonstration I will destroy the disk."

*

"The technicians stopped the camera for several frames to enable them to get excellent photographs, I sent several to the UK Home Secretary, Nathan and he assures me that two of the men were involved with the Fifth Column problem in Liverpool, he says, he is confident they were working for Klaus Gunter, who are they working for now?"

"He has promised to come back to me after Major Goodchild has had time to investigate in Liverpool, one name he has come up with is Boris Bormann; he was defiantly involved in Liverpool."

"Bernie, I have heard the name Goodchild mentioned so many times, shouldn't he be retired by now?"

"Perhaps Harry but he is too valuable to let go, he appears to smell any adverse activity and he has prevented at least three terrorist explosions, he just foils their plots. He lost one side of his face while on the beaches of Dunkirk. He was decorated for his actions on the beaches for keeping discipline with the troops, he appointed two army sergeants to assist him, and they would line the troops up and march them to the seas edge and allocate the numbers the small boats asked for. Had he not done this the troops would have rushed to get on a small boats and they would have capsized, we all have to admit to ourselves, it was a case of individual self preservation. He located a booby trap in the old cinema in Liverpool, it was such a large planted booby trap, had he not found it many people would have perished."

"He sounds such an expert in the field of espionage, I think I will phone Nathan and ask him to allow Major Goodchild to add his expertise to the ticklish problem we have here. I will phone him today."

Later that day Harry told Bernie that Major Goodchild would be joining them in two days time and his wife will be coming with him.

*

When Major Goodchild and his wife Pat arrived at the ranch, Senator Reeves made a point of being there to welcome them. They left the ladies in the lounge and the men into a small room and Harry went right through the information they have at this time.

When he was told about the kidnapping, Lance was quite upset.

"We had a problem similar to this in Liverpool, a good friend of mine had his grandson kidnapped during the Fifth Column business and it devastated my friend Fred."

Bernie was delighted to have Lance working alongside his team.

"I would point out, I am an Intelligence Officer from the UK, so my powers are very limited here, is it possible to have a FBI agent to work with me to ensure that we are all singing from the same song sheet? You will appreciate, the way I work may be unacceptable to your authority but this agent will know to what extent we can approach any problem."

A senior FBI agent arrived at the ranch that evening, he was introduced to Lance and they gelled straight away.

"My name is Lance and you are?"

"I am called Paddy?"

Lance smiled, "Right, Paddy it is."

The following morning there quite a crowd at the breakfast table, the Senator had engaged a chef to be employed at the ranch in view of the number of people staying there.

Bernie explained to Lance and Paddy where the cameras had been installed and how the area was being watched by his agents in a small van full of technical equipment.

Paddy turned to Lance.

"Shall we walk out to the spot that has been chosen by the watchers?"

"Lance, have you got a gun?"

"No, I would not have been allowed to pass the check in desk at Heathrow and board a plane carrying a firearm."

"Right, I will arrange for you to get a gun of your choice while you are here."

When they had finished breakfast, Paddy and Lance about to leave when Bernie said,

"May I join you; two of my team is in that area?"

"Certainly Bernie, we will enjoy your company and of course your expertise."

They started laughing and started to run and fooling about, Ben chased after them. Sophia shouted to Bernie telling him the technicians want to speak to him urgently.

Bernie went back indoors and picked up the phone.

"Hello, this is Colonel Black, speaking."

The technician passed the message.

Bernie caught up with Lance and Paddy.

"May I suggest we walk to the van, the message was that there is some activity where the people stand and watch the house and today there are three men?"

"How far is the van Bernie?"

"Twenty minutes walk."

"Right, let us go to the van and perhaps we can identify the individuals, I wonder why there should be three today watching the house. Perhaps they are plotting to bring the kidnapping plan forward."

Arriving at the van, Bernie introduced Paddy and Lance.

They sat watching the three men with their eyes glued to their binoculars looking in the direction of the house.

Lance pointed to a man on the screen.

"That is Otto Bormann, the man next to him wearing the red baseball cap was involved in trying to burn down a furniture factory in Liverpool and I cannot recall his name. Give me a photograph of that man and I will fax it to my friend Fred Wharton."

A few minutes later the technician handed Lance the photograph.

"Thanks, I will fax it to him tonight."

Chapter 12

Ben organized a dinner party, the Senator had employed a chef and in turn the chef had arranged three waitresses to help with serving the dinner. The chef emphasized that the dinner would be served at eight o'clock and the party should be seated in view of the different menus required.

Ben smiled and said he would ensure they were seated; it was to be drinks at 7-30. He smiled to himself; it is a long time since he had been given an order (except that is of course, excluding his wife). There were 12 people sat around the table.

The meal was a great success, in spite of the various meals required depending on a person's religion.

The chef came to the table when the meal was over to make sure everything had been satisfactory. Ben was so pleased the way the chef had handled the meal; he invited him to join them with a glass of wine, to which, the chef readily agreed.

They were sat around the table talking when a young man entered the room.

He went up to Ben and said,

"I do apologize for my intrusion but I have a most important message for Colonel Black."

Ben just waved his arm indicating where Bernie was sitting.

The young man bent down and spoke to Bernie in Hebrew and then gave him two sheets of foolscap. Bernie just glanced at them, turned them over and laid them on the tabletop. Before the young man left the room, he apologized again to Ben for his intrusion.

*

The men went into a separate room from the ladies to enjoy their cigars and Brandy. Bernie stood up

"Gentlemen, let us get around the table as I want to discuss the message I received this evening.

The fourth man, who we saw arriving on the screen earlier, was delivering a message from the people in charge of the kidnapping children of wealthy parents. It appears they have watched Simon and

Luke go to the stables each evening at nine o'clock, we all know the reason, to give the horses they ride a lump of sugar, that gentlemen is when they intend to strike.

The message that was delivered by the fourth man was instructing the men to lie in wait tomorrow night and when the boys go to the stables they will be overpowered and chloroformed. Down the small embankment at the rear of the stables is a road, not a motorway but what would be classed as an "A" road in the UK and there is a "Lay by" where a car will be waiting to take the boy's away, To where?It is planned to take place tomorrow night. Have any of you got any ideas for us to think about?" Lance raised his hand,

"Right Lance, what are your first thoughts?"

"I would suggest we should over power the driver or drivers who are sat in the car in the lay by and place our own driver in his or her place."

"That is a good idea Lance." Paddy the FBI man joined in.

"Is it a dark area by the stables where they plan to carry out the snatch?"

"I am not sure Paddy, what are you thinking?"

"We have several agents the same or very similar stature as the boys, they could take their place."

"Brilliant Paddy" Bernie looked at the Senator, he nodded.

"So, tonight we will make sure the stable area is in darkness and it will not look different tomorrow night."

The Senator went off to make a phone call, when he returned, he said.

"Tomorrow morning several agents will come for coffee, nothing has been said about the reason for their visit."

"This is a very delicate situation, we do not know what or who we are up against, if they are anything like the people we came up against in Liverpool, be very, very careful. I was investigating some people in the UK before I came here and it transpires that the dream of the Third Reich controlling Europe is still alive and the money from the kidnapping is going into the coffers to keep this dream alive. This is not the only country where this is happening, Brazil has recently experienced a spate of kidnapping and the amount of the ransom asked for the return of the children was unbelievable.

The man on the screen we did not recognize at first, was a very active member of the group of Ex Nazi Officers who organized the arson attack on a furniture store in Liverpool, his name is Heine Schmitt and he is a very wicked and vicious man, if you should come up against him, shoot first. I am not trying to alarm you gentlemen but I have had first hand dealings with these men. That is why I earnestly ask you to be careful." Lance sat down.

"Thank you, Lance."

*

The following morning several cars pulled up outside the main door of the ranch. Nat greeted them and took them to the stable area, the stable hands brought out the horses from their stalls walking them round the yard and the group of FBI agents was joined by the Senator and his team, including Simon and Luke, they tried to impress the visitors with their new found knowledge. The group walked round as if inspecting the Bloodstock, one horse every one was taken with was Tilley, they all said she was a magnificent looking horse but Ben told them, Tilley was a chaser not a leader.

After a while, they all went into the ranch for coffee; the agents were a little non-plussed as to what was happening.

The two agents who were most like the boys were taken to one side and instructed to stay behind and hand their car keys over to two of Bernie's men and they will drive the cars away making it look as if all of the visitors have left.

The two agents were taken into a separate room to be briefed by the Senator, he explained to them the plan the watchers have and the plans he is working on. Having told them what part of the plan they are to play, one of the agents looked up.

"What are we to do, retaliate when they try to chloroform us, or just go along with the kidnapping? If they are as vicious as Lance has told us, when they realize they have been duped, they will shoot us."

The Senator sat rubbing his chin.

"We hadn't considered that possibility; we must give more thought to this problem." Paddy glanced at Lance.

"We had overlooked this, do we intervene when the agents are attacked at the stables or let them put them in the car, bearing in mind it will be our driver?" Lance looked up, "Can I run this idea past you?"

"When the people strike to overpower the boys, or should I say the agents, arrest and handcuff them, put a coat over the heads of the agents and our people take them to the car and sit with them. The driver will take them to the house where the are to be kept prisoners until the ransom is paid but when they arrive at the house our agents can make a move, arresting or if it becomes a dangerous situation shoot them, they must not take any chances. Just one thing, the car and the agents must be tagged with a homing device to enable the control van to pin point their position to safeguard our agents."

"I like the way you ensure the safety of our own people Lance," said the Senator smiling.

"I think it might just work, I would like to discuss this plan with Bernie and Ben."

After a while Ben, Bernie and the Senator came out a room and told the team that they had decided to go ahead with the latest plan Lance had suggested.

"Isaac is going to speak to the boys and explain they must not under any circumstances go near the stables this evening."

Luke and Simon promised to do as their father said but they decided to take the knobs of sugar to their mounts much earlier. Luke turned to Simon,

"The grown up's are always telling us what to do, they claim to know what is best for us."

Eight thirty, dinner was finished and they all sat in the lounge watching the TV. Sadie looked up saying.

"It is wonderful to have company, it can be very lonely here, the nearest neighbour is half a mile away, impossible to drop in for a cup of tea and have a good gossip.

Where have the boys?"

"They have gone to their room to plays games on their TV."

Quarter to nine Bernie sent his team to take their places as planned and bang on nine o'clock the two agents went to the stables and proceeded to give the horses the sugar, every one was keyed up but nothing happened. The agents stayed in the stables for a while but still nobody was about, they walked to the rear of the stables and they could see there was no car in the lay by. The two agents went back into the house and reported to Bernie, Lance said to Bernie.

"Have we got the wrong night?"

Go upstairs and ask the boys to come down into the lounge and I will explain why their father insisted that they did not go to the stables tonight."

Paddy came jumping down the stairs two steps at a time,

"They are not in their room."

"Don't panic, check through the house and the stables."

The premises were searched the boys could not be found. Ben was livid.

"Isaac, did you tell them how important it was that they should listen to you?"

"I emphasized that they must not go any where near the stables this evening."

There came a knock on the room door.

"May I speak to Colonel Black?"

"Yes, come in."

"Oh! Hello Max."

"My children don't always do as I ask and I wondered about Luke and Simon. I took the liberty of putting a homing tag inside the sole of their trainers."

"Well done Max, this might be the life saver; did you note the number of the tags you used?"

"Yes, shall I take the numbers to the van, as they will indicate the frequency for their equipment to operate on?"

"Do it straight away and thank you Max; I suppose we should thank your children for misbehaving on occasion."

*

Bernie, Paddy and Lance went straight to the van which contained the technical equipment; Max had given the senior technician the numbers printed on the homing tags. His team was scanning the screen hoping to find the location of the tags, they all sat with a cup of coffee while the scanning took place, and suddenly a cheer went up, got it!

The chips in the boy's trainers were found, after a little adjustment they pin pointed the exact spot where the boys are being held. They studied the maps and identified the house where the boys are imprisoned.

Bernie immediately phoned one of his team leaders giving him the map reference of the house, he instructed that no action is taken but I would like to know the full details of the building, is it a large or small house, what is the security and is it guarded by people or dogs? I want photographs by the morning; in fact, I want to know everything about the place.

The most important thing Rueben: the occupants and who are these people in charge of such a large scale operation. As Bernie put the phone down, Paddy said.

"With respect Colonel Black, this is now an FBI operation. In this country we regard kidnapping to be a capital charge, when they are caught, charged and if found guilty they will face the death sentence." Bernie smiled.

"I realize what you say is true but my team is so experienced with these situations don't you underestimate their capabilities."

"They might be experienced in this type of situation but your people have no authority what so ever. They themselves might end up in front of a judge."

"What he is saying is quite right Bernie." said the Senator.

Bernie again contacted his team leaders and explained the whole story and he told them, if they saw any part of the operation going wrong, step in. I will accept full responsibility.

*

The FBI men surrounded the house remaining under cover but they were a little unsure of the next step was to be, they had been told about the two boys being held hostage in the house, that is all they knew.

Paddy arrived at the house and called all the agents together.

"We will not be attacking the place, just wait and hope one of the men will walk out into the garden for fresh air or to have a cigarette. If one does step outside the building, overpower him, handcuff him and a car will take him away."

The agents went back to their positions to watch the doors front and back and one of the occupants did walk out of the house and he wandered into the garden. Two of the agents did as they had been told to do, handcuff him and marched him to another group who bundled him into a car and whisked him off to be interrogated.

At first he refused to talk but he could see his refusal to talk was futile. He told them there were five men left in the house and the boys were in small room at the back of the house on the first floor. When asked about the people inside the house, he told them, two of the men he had never seen before and didn't know their names.

One man in the house could not understand where his pal had got to; he asked if he could go out and look for him, the man in charge nodded and he came outside.

He went into the garden calling his friends name, he received no reply, so he walked further into the garden, which, was his downfall and two agents pulled him to the ground and handcuffed him. This man was then transported to join his pal, under arrest. Paddy could not resist telling them they had committed a capital offence which carries the death penalty. The men's faces went a deathly white.

"Why, we only did as we were told?"

"Who gave you the order?"

"We have no idea; we were employed to drive the cars to rescue the two boys away from some pedophiles."

The man in charge is over six feet tall, well built and he has a black eye patch over his right eye and he is German and his own man is afraid of him that is all we can tell you."

"Right, now draw a diagram of the lay out inside the house indicating where the boy's are being kept."

"Are they friends of yours?"

"Yes, they were the one's who were approached in the first place to rescue the boys."

"If you went back into the house, could you persuade them to release the boys without the German's being aware?"

"I honestly do not know the answer to your question."

"You think about it for a while."

Paddy and Lance left the cell making sure it was securely locked and drove back to the house to join the surveillance team

Paddy turned to Lance.

"What do you think we should do now?"

Lance suggested they should bide their time and watch for any further developments.

In the distance a car was spotted coming towards the house, they all moved back in the bushes so as not to be seen. It was a large black limousine and it came down the drive and came to a halt outside the heavy looking wooden door at the front of the house.

The car door opened and a heavily built man accompanied by two other men went to the main door, he was greeted as if he was royalty. They remained in the house for ten minutes, they came out of the house and got back into the car but it was five people who came out of the house and got into the car and drove off.

Paddy noted the number plate and contacted his office instructing the car and the occupants to be apprehended and taken to a local law office to be interrogated, under no circumstances are they to be released without my say so.

The car was stopped and the passengers were taken to the police station. The big man shouted at the desk Sheriff who was asking questions to complete a form.

"I am visiting the USA with a trade delegation, so any violation of your traffic laws does not affect me, as an envoy I claim immunity."

The officer would have none of it and he instructed that all five should be placed in a cell until the FBI chief arrives.

*

Bernie asked to be allowed to join Paddy and Lance to go to the Sheriff's office; Paddy was pleased to have Bernie along. Bernie was quite intrigued that such a powerful industrialist should be involved in kidnapping on such a large scale?

When Bernie approached the cell containing Frank Von Kessler, he stood up, clicked his heels together, raised his right arm shouting "Hiel Hitler" refusing to shake Bernie's offered hand but looked at him with hatred in his eyes.

Lance walked with Paddy down the cells; one man looked through the bars saying.

"Good God, not you."

"Yes Klaus Gunter, it is I, Major Goodchild."

Klaus shouted through the bars of the cell.

"This is the man who framed Heine with false evidence, to get him imprisoned for life."

"Your friend should have been hanged for all the terrible atrocities he ordered to be carried out in France during the war, which you lost. Still, the ten members of the French resistance group he had their legs machine gunned and left crawling on the floor had their own back when they shattered his legs with gunfire after the trial. Is he coping with his wheelchair okay Klaus?"

*

Before they left, Paddy told the sheriff that he wanted a statement from each of his prisoners. I need to know, why were they at the house, why had they kidnapped the boys and from where did they get the black Mercedes limousine. Did they hire the car, if so from which company and who paid for the hire?

The sheriff smiled.

"It looks like being an interesting next few hours sir."

They went back to watch the house but there was no activity, Paddy decided to send one of the two men they had captured back into the house. He instructed the man to go into the house, check if all the German's had left, if so, tell your friends what I told you earlier, kidnapping is a capital offence which carries the death penalty.

The man was taken back to the garden where he had been snatched from.

"Where the hell have you been Max?"

"I was captured when I went out for a smoke but they have released me to explain to you the penalty for your action."

"Where are the German's?"

"They left a while back saying they would return in a couple of hours."

"Did they take the boys with them?"

"No, they are still locked in the small bedroom."

"Max, we did not kidnap the two boys, as I understand; we rescued them from the pedophiles."

"That is not true Tommy, they would be held here until a ransom had been paid."

"I told you I was arrested by the FBI when I went out for a smoke, if we release the boys now we can leave without being charged."

They quickly decided to release the boys and scarper.

When Simon and Luke walked out of the front door, they looked up and saw Lance they ran over to him and they were both in tears. After a minute or two they wiped their eyes.

"Please don't tell our father we cried."

"Not at all son, I think you have both been very brave, your captors are very vicious men."

Sadie and Isaac were very pleased to get the boys back home with them. Both Sadie and Lottie were crying.

Bernie waited at the house after Paddy and Lance had left with the boys, the men came out of the back door, he shouted; "You did the best thing, off you go."

*

The following morning Paddy asked Bernie and Lance if they would like to go with him to the sheriff's office where Klaus was being held. Paddy was anxious to read the statements.

When they arrived the sheriff shouted.

"Good Morning."

"Good Morning sheriff, I am anxious to read the statements."

"You will be disappointed."

"Why, what do you mean?"

"One hour after you left yesterday, several FBI and CIA agents arrived with a release letter from the Presidents office, it said the men were not to be charged and some influential people in the Whitehouse had sent the agents to ensure their release and take them to board a plane for Germany, flying from a local airport."

The sheriff scratched his head.

"Very strange situation, sir."

Paddy phoned Ben.

"Is Senator Reeves still at the ranch?"

"No, he left some time ago."

Paddy explained briefly what had taken place and Ben was very annoyed

"I will not ring him Paddy, I think it will be better coming from you as a FBI agent, I would have thought that you should have been contacted, it is your case."

When they arrived back at the ranch Paddy telephoned the Senator.

"Paddy, I know nothing about the prisoners not being charged and released. I will make it my business to find out."

During the evening the Senator did ring back.

"Paddy, I have not made any progress, everyone I approach does not know about the situation, those who did would not discuss it. I will find out, I have a very close friend who is an advisor in the Whitehouse. I will contact you when I can finally get an answer."

Bernie and Lance were both very upset about the whole business, Lance turned to Bernie.

"Who is so high up in this government that they can quash any charges being put against people who have broken the law of this country and assist them to escape by plane. The plane landed at the International Airport Tegel in Berlin and on arrival they were met by a chauffeur-driven limousine, this information was sent by one of your agents.

*

The following morning, Paddy asked Bernie and Lance to join him. "All three of us have been called to the Whitehouse, what are we to answer for, I don't know but whatever it is we have to go."

The following day a government car called to transport them to the local airport and they were put on a plane destine for Washington. On arrival in Washington a car was waiting to take them to keep their appointment. They were escorted from the car to a small room just inside the main door and they were offered coffee, tea and alcoholic drinks of their choice.

Ten minutes later a young man into the room asking them to follow him and he took them to a large room.

The room was very elaborate and expensively decorated. There was a long highly polished table with five men sitting round it; one sat at the head of the table and two either side. All five were impeccably groomed and they each had a distinguished presence about them. The man at the head of the table looked up and smiled and he said.

"Allow me to introduce myself to you, I am the Vice President of the USA and these gentlemen are the chiefs of staff of our security forces. I will address Paddy as he is one of our senior agents, kindly give a briefing of what has happened over this kidnapping escapade."

*

Paddy outlined how they found out the kidnappers plan was and when they intended to strike.

"Our plans went wrong when the boys disobeyed their father and they were captured. Fortunately a tracking device had been implanted in one of the boy's trainer and we were able to locate the boy's location.

We captured two of their team when the first man came out of the house for a smoke and the second when he came out looking for his pal.

During our watch a car came to the house and collected several of the Germans, the number plate was noted and the car was apprehended and the occupants arrested and imprisoned. They were left in prison and the sheriff was instructed to obtain statements from each prisoner but when we called the following morning, they had been released by authority of this department and the CIA and FBI agents escorted them to a plane at the local airport. The letter authorizing their release was from this office and signed."

"The letter authorizing the release of the prisoners from the sheriff's office did not come from this office, tests have been carried out and we have found that the letter heading and the paper was authentic but the signature is a mystery but it doesn't belong to any of my office personnel.

Gentlemen, we have been had, some clever person had the letter, the FBI and the CIA agents cooperated on the strength of the letter which was supposed to have originated from this office. How or by whom, I do not know yet but you may rest assured we will get to the bottom of this fiasco.

I do apologize to you gentlemen for being misled by the clever plan after you have worked so hard to prevent such an incident.

I respect your confidence by not repeating what I have told you."

"Before we go any further, one thing puzzles me.

How was Klaus Gunter allowed to enter this country?

Had he applied for a visa through the normal channels, it would not have been issued."

"The first priority is to find who allowed Gunter to enter this country." Lance looked up and smiled.

"It must be the same American group of people who used their influence to get all War Crime charges against Gunter to be dropped and in consequence, he did not stand trial in Nuremburg along with his colleagues, who were convicted and hanged. This matter was investigated but thwarted by officialdom."

"Thank you for that piece of information, I was not aware this had happened. Have you any names to check back on?"

"I haven't but my immediate boss, Ken Lee has a complete file, you have the authority to request the file but I haven't."

"Does he work for Nathan?"

"Yes, he operates from Nathan's office."

"The more I hear, the more I realize our security is not as tight as it should be.

"Thank you for your time gentlemen, I would like all of you to stay for dinner, my secretary will arrange accommodation tonight. Will that be okay with you?"

They all nodded.

A young lady entered the room.

"This is my secretary Lucy, go along with her and she will take to your hotel, anything you need, the hotel porter will get for you as you may not have come prepared to stay. A car will pick you up at the hotel at eight o'clock to bring you here for dinner."

They were taken by car to a very plush hotel; they were shown to their rooms before parting they arranged to meet in the bar.

When they had showered and made any phone calls, they did meet in the hotel bar, Bernie smiled at Lance.

"I like the treatment."

"I couldn't agree more."

CHAPTER 13

Nathan, the home secretary and Peter Horne received a phone call asking them to report to a castle in the north of France. They again decided not to use a government car, they decided to hire one when they had crossed the channel. On arrival at the castle they found they were the last to arrive and refreshments were made available and they were able to rest for a while.

Jan Von Krupp came out of the conference room and invited the six ministers to join him.

He waited until they were all settled before speaking.

"Gentlemen, I hope the fact we have kept our head down for a few months, our enemy will have lowered their guard.

No doubt you will have heard about the kidnap attempt, to snatch Isaac's two boys, fortunately their efforts were thwarted.

I have the cards ready to deal as before."

Jan dealt the cards around the table it was noticeable how the sighs of relief were heard as people picked up their card, looking across at Henri Girard's face it was obvious that he had collected the Ace of Spades.

Nathan was curious, they all guessed that Henri was the only person who had not carried out elimination and he was the one to get the ace, contrary to what Jan said, he knows who is dealing with the elimination.

Jan picked up a little black bag, pointing to a man sat to his right and asked him to pick a slip of paper from the bag. He pulled out a name and handed to Jan. He unfolded the piece of paper.

"The man selected, is, General Bruno Rossi, a retired Italian officer."

Jan went to his brief case and pulled out a file.

*

"General Rossi was in charge of the tank divisions when Benito Mussolini ordered the invasion of Abyssinia in 1935.

The Emperor Haile Selassie appealed to the world for help but all the United Nations did was to place a partial embargo on Italy. How he came to have been invited to the meeting to decide on how to take over Europe I don't know.

Bruno, being such a vicious man was put in charge of putting down any uprising by the Abyssinians against the Italian invaders. Any riots that took place, the rioters were shot, no arrests or trials, just shot dead.

Perhaps it was because of his viciousness that Klaus Gunter thought he would be a suitable General to help their plans to succeed."

"He would have the young boys accused of rioting lined up and he would walk up and down the lines of these young men looking them in the face, when he saw fear in the eyes of a young man, he would have him taken to his quarters.

Later he would sexually abuse this young man and then to amuse himself further he would torture and physically abuse him.

This happened on numerous occasions, in fact, several young men committed suicide rather than face the ordeal again. His senior officers knew what was happening and they took no action as they were conducting their own lives, in a similar manner.

Bruno is living in Florence, he was married with a daughter but his marriage did not last long as he lost interest in his wife and they separated, he still prefers the company of young boys.

He was in charge of several tank divisions in North Africa in World War11 and his atrocities were vile. He was known to have any prisoners taken shot, claiming that he did not have the troops to guard them or the food to feed them."

*

Henri discussed his problem with two of his close colleagues, it was decided to each compile a dossier on Bruno's daily movements. Three weeks later they met up in a hotel room which Henri has reserved to discuss their findings. Henri had booked the room to avoid prying eyes or people listening. They each laid their sheets of paper out on a table, each sheet was very similar. The one thing they all highlighted was on a Sunday morning Bruno would ride his powerful motorbike up and down the motorway at a very high speed. Henri's deputy came up with an idea, which, they all agreed with.

The idea was to loosen the oil drain plug of the gear box, hoping this will cause a problem.

Henri contacted a young engineer and offered to pay him handsomely to carry out the job. He agreed to do the job but refused to accept any money, his cousin had been one of Bruno's young boys and he had committed suicide rather than face another session with Bruno.

The engineer carried out the plan on the Saturday; he left the drain plug just on one turn of the thread. The plan was successful; Bruno's death was announced in the local and national papers.

A coroner's enquiry was held and several engineering experts were called to be questioned. The coroner listened to all the experts and finally addressed the family and friends who were present.

"I am of the opinion, that due to the very high speed Bruno Rossi was travelling it caused vibration, which loosened the oil plug and the heat thinned the oil, which, escaped through the threads and caused the plug to drop off.

The workings of the gears in the gearbox became overheated and through friction without any lubrication expanded the lay shaft which seized, locking the rear wheel, Bruno was catapulted off the motor cycle and he landed in the path of an oncoming lorry and his death was instantaneous.

My findings in this case are that Bruno Rossi's death was an accident with no other person involved."

When Henri read the report he contacted the Telegraph Newspaper to report that the Smith family had lost another of its members.

*

Jan Von Krupp arranged a meeting, which, was to be attended in a Hotel in the south of France. He suggested that the ministers should take their wives or partners and the ministers could attend the meetings while the ladies visited the beautiful shops in that area.

Nathan was a little unsure whether his wife would enjoy such a trip but when he mentioned it to her, she said that she could pack her case in ten minutes.

Nathan received a phone call from Peter saying his wife was looking forward to the trip; in fact, her entire wardrobe is laid out on the bed, she is trying to decide what to pack.

This made Nathan chuckle, he knew he would face a similar operation taking place in his bedroom.

Jan had ensured them it was a top class hotel.

The ministers and their wives arrived at the Grand Hotel, it was Grand and it was really a luxury hotel. Olga, Nathan's wife, really enjoyed the ambiance.

The dinner was excellent and the ladies enjoyed the attention paid to them by the waiters and waitresses.

The meeting was to be held the following morning; the ladies were taken by car to the shopping area while the ministers went into a small meeting room. As they entered the room they were assured, that the room had been swept for any listening bugs or small cameras.

"Gentlemen, as you will have read in the Telegraph, Bruno Rossi was sadly killed in a road accident while riding his motorcycle on the motorway in Florence.

There are now four names left on the list but I would like to propose that the name of Walther Frank should be removed from the list. The interview that was published was entirely true; he helped a lot of children to escape the Gestapo's scourge. I have had Walther thoroughly investigated and he did save the lives of many people not only children from the basement of the house, which, was set up by several religious leaders."

The ministers all agreed that Walther's name should be removed from the list.

"Thank you gentlemen, I'm glad you all agree."

When the ladies returned from their shopping trip they were all very excited and Nathan looked at Peter and then the big shopping bags, they both shrugged their shoulders and smiled.

Before they left the hotel Jan said that he was arranging a meeting in a hotel in Hastings in the UK but would contact them with the details.

*

Several weeks later Jan sent out the date and at which hotel in Hastings the meeting would be held. Nathan and Peter were delighted that the meeting was to be held in their own country for a change.

When they arrived at the hotel, they were met by a team of security people who were busy checking the security and the bugs. They were told to go to the bar whilst the investigation was being carried out, a rumour was circulating that the hotel had been infiltrated by people who were closing in on the vigilantes.

Nathan knew of the scare and had organized the security check but he had not mentioned it to any one that the tip off came from his boss, the Prime Minister, so how had that rumour started. The tip off came from a source in Hungary, why from there, Nathan could not understand and how did they know of the meetings.

Later that afternoon the man in charge of the security team asked to speak to Jan and Nathan in private, they went into another room. He turned to Nathan.

"We have found a small explosive device, which, has been removed and taken away and a small recording camera, which, had been made in this country.

May I suggest?

You all go into the bar area and we will check right through again, just in case some clever devil has placed a device in an area after we checked."

One hour later he gave Jan the nod and Jan invited the ministers back into the room.

"Gentlemen, I do not intend dealing the cards today, the reason I wanted to speak to you all is about some recent information we have and I feel it should be shared with you."

"When I read the dossier on Otto in Brazil, I told you that he received a substantial monthly income, from where or from whom we did not know.

I can now tell you we have unearthed the source.

The Nazi regime accumulated large sums of money, either from plunder or Swiss account numbers obtained from their victims after being tortured. The investigators were confident that all the Swiss account numbers were passed to a central pool. They reckoned that the hierarchy of the Nazi movement passed their own bank numbers in case of their death. Personally, I am of the opinion that this would be most unlikely, as their own family would be denied of any wealth they had accumulated over the years.

The man who is in control the money and is the paymaster of this massive fortune in the Swiss accounts is Gustav Reimer; he runs a small cigarette and cigar shop in Bavaria. He is a most insignificant looking man, short, fat and scruffy; in fact, he could be mistaken for a homeless person, maybe this was the reason he was allocated the job. He must have a brilliant brain, to deal with such vast sums of money and distributing the correct amount to different people.

We are given to understand; that if any of the Nazi Party became domicile in another country rather than face the Nuremberg trials, he or she would receive a monthly income and the amount they receive is dependant on the rank they held in the party.

I am not aware the amount that is paid out each month to these people but the amount held in the account is so vast that not one banker will enter into discussion regarding the amount of money. The investigators are trying to discover the method used to transfer these funds, when we do, we shall try to stop them."

"Thank you gentlemen for bearing with me but I felt that you all should be made aware of any new developments."

*

They went back into the bar area where a light tea had been prepared. They drifted off in pairs, transport and flights home had all been arranged for them. Nathan's chauffeured car pulled up at the main door to drive Peter and Nathan home.

Nathan's wife was pleased to have him back home, prior to his leaving she was conscious of the unusual telephone activity, something was just not right and she had been worried.

After dinner, they both sat back relaxing and enjoying the television, in fact, it was a most pleasant evening.

That was until the ten o'clock news came on; one of top news items was showing a hotel on fire, which, the commentator said was a ranging inferno due to a massive explosion. Fortunately the hotel owners had taken most of the staff and the residents by coach to the local theatre earlier but the barman and a waitress were badly injured.

Nathan said nothing but his face looked drained and went deathly white, when he looked up his wife was crying.

"Why must you keep putting yourself in the firing line Nathan?"

The phone started to ring and Olga picked up the receiver, she said "Certainly"

"Nathan, it is the Prime Minister"

"Nathan, the hotel was contacted and we requested rooms for you all to stay overnight. The bomber was thrown off course but it didn't help the other poor souls."

"Thanks, have we a mole?"

"You have, I would contact Ken and Major Lance Goodchild and I feel sure they will find the undercover person but it is up to you. Cheerio for now Nathan, I am pleased you are safe."

The following morning when Nathan had cleared all the outstanding correspondence off his office desk, he asked his secretary to ask both Ken and Lance to report to his office.

Chapter 14

Ken arrived first and when Nathan's secretary showed Ken into Nathan's office, he looked up and asked his young lady to make some coffee.

"Thanks for coming Ken, I have contacted Lance and he should be here shortly, in the meantime we will have a coffee. I won't explain why I asked you to come along until Lance arrives, it will save me going through all the details twice."

His secretary brought the coffee into his office and Lance came into the office with her.

"Thanks for coming so promptly Lance, now you are both here I will explain the problem. You both know the group I have been working with and you have helped in the past, this time it is not so dangerous, at least I don't think so.

I was to attend a meeting in a hotel in Hastings, just before I left home I received a phone call from the PM, he had a tip off from the Hungarian secret police that the terrorist intended to attack the hotel during the meeting.

I contacted our security people and they carried out a complete sweep through the hotel, they found one explosive device and dealt with it but while the meeting was taking place the PM telephoned the hotel asking them to arrange rooms to enable all the people at the meeting to stay overnight but we had no intention of staying.

At nine thirty that evening a very powerful bomb exploded, it had been placed between the dining area and the bar, the most vulnerable position had we stayed in the hotel; no doubt you saw the blazing inferno on the news last night."

"Good lord, was that the hotel the meeting was held?"

"Yes, we were very lucky to have left earlier."

"I would like you both to try and find the mole, it is obvious that the PM's phone call had been intercepted and passed on. I appreciate, this could be a very difficult task but I hope you and your teams will take this project on. You can put any other jobs you have on the back burner, if what you dealing with it important, pass it on to another agent. Any problems refer them to me."

*

Nathan had arranged with Peter to come to his office the following morning and then they can discuss how they will approach the task ahead.

The following day Peter arrived bright and early, they sat down toying with suggestions put on the table but they were not happy with any of their ideas and they broke off and went out to a local coffee bar hoping to get an inspiration away from the office but neither could think straight.

Arriving back at the office, they both agreed to ask Nathan's undercover team to get the CCTV films from the sea ports and the airports covering the days before the hotel explosion, hoping they can pick out any known or suspected terrorists.

Ken and Lance joined them and each sat studying the films, suddenly, Lance shouted.

"Bingo: this man is Karl Kayberg, he was one of the leading lights in Liverpool, he did the organizing of the nasty jobs and how the hell has he been allowed back into this country?"

One man sat with Lance jumped.

"The man next to him is Abdul Mohamed, he was born in this country but he has been to Pakistan several times to go on the training courses. We couldn't understand how we lost him off our screen but he is back, he needs watching, we were positive he was responsible for several UK explosions but couldn't prove it.

He always travels on a false passport, immigration people had been alerted to watch for him but it is obvious they have failed in their duty.

Now we will have to find him to keep an eye on him."

"From what you say, he could be the explosives man we are looking for."

There a knock on Nathan's office door and his secretary entered the room.

"There is a gentleman on the telephone wishing to speak to you sir, privately, I have transferred the call to the small office."

"Thank you, Mrs. Bird."

Nathan left the room and went into the small office and picked up the phone.

"Hello, this is the Home Secretary."

"Hi! Nathan, I am so glad you are safe and well.

This is Bernie, can we meet, or I can come to your office?"

"You are welcome to join me in my office; I will make sure we are alone."

"Is it possible to get Ken and Lance to join us and of course Peter?"

"Certainly, when is it convenient for you?"

"I am phoning you from a phone box in the next street from your office, if I came now could you get Ken and Lance to join us?"

"They are both in my office now; I look forward to seeing you shortly."

Nathan went back into his office and he turned to the members of his team asking them to leave.

When his team had left he told the others that Bernie would be joining them in a few minutes, as he said that, a knock on the door and his secretary showed Bernie into the room.

After all the greetings were over, Bernie looked at the spools of films that was lying around and smiled.

"Have you found any person you suspect?"

Lance pointed out Karl Kayberg and Abdul standing next to him. Bernie turned to Lance saying.

"Abdul flew into Glasgow, he left there on a plane for Leeds and Bradford, he went on from there to Heathrow but you still picked

him up, good.

He is in Slough at present but my team is confident that he was responsible for the Hastings explosion.

One of my team found out about the Hastings job, I telephoned your PM but he was told the tipoff came from the Hungarian secret police, had I told him it was I, he would have taken no action.

I'll tell why, two months ago I told him of a terrorist plot in London and he stepped up the security but nothing happened and he stood them down. The devastating bombing attack took place three days later and he blamed me for getting the wrong information but as in the Hastings case, someone had intercepted the phone call and changed the timing of the attack."

"Nathan looked quite perturbed, so there is a mole in the P.M's office."

"I would say it is 100% the case."

Nathan went to a large cupboard in his office and brought out a bottle of malt whisky.

"Shall we enjoy a drink before we scratch our heads and try to seek this problem out?"

"What a wonderful idea." said Peter, smiling. Bernie looked at Nathan.

"Have you got the film from the hotel CCTV camera and the list of people who stayed at the hotel several days before the meeting or were they destroyed?"

"No I haven't, I should have thought of that, I will send for it now."

With that, Nathan left the room and went into the secretary's room and instructed her to contact one of his team and send him to the hotel in Hastings for the ledger and the film.

Several hours later the agent rang to say, both the records and the film had been destroyed in the fire.

Nathan telephoned Downing Street requesting an appointment with the Prime Minister, the PM's secretary arranged an appointment for him at 4o'clock.

*

Arriving, Nathan was shown into the P.M'S office.

"Hello Nathan, have you come in a government car being driven?"

"Yes."

"Good, what would you like to drink?"

"Scotch on the rocks, will do fine."

Right, he poured out the drinks and handed a glass to Nathan.

"Cheers, I am so pleased that you left the hotel before the explosion, it was a gamble.

I phoned the hotel asking them to arrange accommodation for you and your friends overnight, I felt sure the bomber would leave it to later time when the hotel was making the arrangements for you to stay."

"How many incoming and outgoing phone lines do you have manned?"

"Five, normally."

"Is it possible for your security men to forward the history files of each of your telegraphists to my office, whether they were on duty on that day or not but attach a memo indicating who was on duty when you made the hotel booking. Also who was on duty when Bernie advised of a terrorist attack which was changed after you stood the alert people down?"

"Yes Nathan, the files will be sent to your office, in fact, I'll deal with it myself, I'll know then nothing has been tampered with."

"Thank you sir, I'll call on you when I have any positive information on the leaks."

They shook hands and Nathan went out to his car and was driven away.

Major Lance Goodchild asked permission to send one of his security teams to do a complete sweep of the communication system in the building.

The team spent two days going from room to room hoping to find a lapse in the security system but they found nothing and the search was called off.

Lance and Ken decided to go into number 10 to snoop around themselves, when they sought permission, it was granted immediately.

They spent best part of a day checking and they could not find any phone taps or listening bugs, which, the security had drawn, a blank.

Lance knocked on the PM's office door.

"Come in."

They went in and told him that they too had drawn a blank.

Lance casually glanced up at the ceiling and his eyes were drawn to one of the white plastic clips used to pin the telephone wire to the picture rail. He felt confident that the clip in question was larger than the rest, Lance put his fingers to his lips, indicating silence and guided the PM and Ken out of the office.

"Sir, I may be wrong but I would like our technicians to check one of the plastic clips, it looks larger than the rest."

The PM did not reply he just nodded.

Lance left the room and telephoned his office asking his secretary to contact Dennis their technician.

Three minutes later Lance received a message, to the effect that Dennis would be with him in thirty minutes depending on the traffic conditions.

The PM took them into the board room and offered Ken and Lance a drink.

"The world is your oyster! You can have tea, coffee or scotch on the rocks," they all decided on the latter. They sat chatting about the world affairs enjoying their drinks; one of the secretaries entered the room.

"Excuse me sir but a young gentleman is in the hall asking to speak to Major Goodchild."

Lance left the room and when he saw the young man, he said.

"Thanks for coming so quickly Dennis, I'll show you what I want you to do, he then explained about the larger plastic clip, it could be suspect or I could be completely wrong."

"Can you tell without dismantling or removing?"

"I'm sure I can."

Lance took Dennis into the boardroom and introduced him to the PM and Ken.

"Now sir, have I your permission to take this young man into your office?"

"Certainly, we will come with you."

They went into the office; Dennis looked up at the plastic clip.

"I will get my small step ladder and instruments."

Dennis arranged his steps and checked the clip with one of his instruments.

"Is it possible for your office to receive a call and you speak to the caller?"

Lance phoned his office asking his secretary to ring him on the special number he gave to her.

"You can tell the girl on the switchboard that this call is expected, she should then put you straight through."

Several minutes later the PM's phone started to ring; he picked it up and handed it to Lance, who in turn nodded to Dennis. Lance chatted to his secretary discussing the files which Lance knew she was working on. After a few minutes he said.

"Cheerio."

Dennis looked at Lance and nodded.

"You were right sir, it is a small transmitter and it is set at a certain frequency to transmit any conversation to a receiver within a 10 mile range."

The PM was devastated.

"Isn't any thing safe today?"

"Dennis, can you tweak the frequency off the station a little, which would need the transmitter to be adjusted or replaced?"

"Yes, I can adjust it, then the transmitter would have to be recalibrated or replaced, is that what you want doing?"

"Do that Dennis and fit a small camera covering the clip transmitter, hopefully it will put on film him, or her or whoever comes into the office to carry out the repairs."

The PM was very upset about the whole business.

"The person who fitted the transmitter in my office could have easily placed a bomb."

He picked up the phone and told Nathan to report to his office immediately.

"Dennis, have you been cleared by the security people?"

"Yes sir, Major Goodchild will vouch for me."

"Dennis has worked on all sensitive problems in the government with me?"

"Thanks, Lance. While you are dealing with this matter, I shall carry on with my work in the underground office."

*

Nathan was surprised to be summoned to the PM's office so urgently and he wondered how the situation could have changed in the two hours since he was with the PM.

On arrival to the Downing Street office, he was shown into the cabinet room and the PM joined him several minutes later.

"Nathan, we have a problem at this address, the technical boys came armed with all the latest equipment to pinpoint a leakage in our communication system but they drew a blank. I invited Ken and Lance into my office and within five minutes Lance pinpointed the small transmitter in the form of a white plastic pin securing the telephone wire to the picture frame. The telephone wires are kept visible to prevent them being tapped unnoticed.

One of your technicians checked and the transmitter has a range of ten miles.

I would like Major Goodchild to remain in this building until we have had every avenue thoroughly checked, not only the instruments but the staff also. He is more efficient than the sniffer dogs."

They both laughed.

"I'll have a word with Lance and I know he will be delighted to get his teeth into this problem."

They shook hands and Nathan left the room and sought out Lance.

When he found Lance, he was up a ladder; he and Dennis were checking some old disused cables in the roof cavity and Lance decided they should be removed.

"Lance, the PM wants you to remain here until this situation has been resolved."

"How on earth did you spot the plastic clip being a different size, were you looking for any such bug?"

"I just happened to look up at the ceiling and it just struck me, must be my good eyesight and loads of good luck."

Lance's face broke into a large grin.

They shook hands and Nathan left the building.

Lance went to the main office and asked if he could speak to the gentleman in charge of the building maintenance, he was directed to an office. He knocked on the door, a voice called.

"Enter."

The man at the desk had several large sheets of plans on the desk in front of him.

"Hello, how can I help you sir?"

"My name is Lance Goodchild and I am here to clear out the threat of any listening bugs."

"I'm John Firth, I am in charge of any building repairs and arranging decorators should any work be decided on.

The people engaged to work in this building are vetted first."

Lance turned to the man;

"We will be working together for a while. My name is Lance and you are John, are you comfortable with that?"

"Yes Lance, I am more than comfortable, it is like a breath of fresh air to speak to someone who is down to earth and not a pretentious self important pompous person."

"John, can you give me a list of people who has worked in this building over the past two months?"

"Yes, I can have the lists ready in about one hour, the budget is so tight and I have to keep a tight rein on any expenditure, although I don't always use the cheapest tender. Some companies are more expensive but they do a better job?"

"Thinking about it Lance, I wonder if the people who deliver the materials have been vetted?"

"I would like your electrician to work with our technician to remove any old cables which he thinks are suspect."

"Yes, I will arrange that for you."

John came down the corridor with a young man dressed in a boiler suit.

"Lance, this is our electrician Eric. He has been through all the necessary checks to enable him to work in the Prime Ministers rooms."

"Right Eric, I am Lance and this is Dennis." Dennis had just come down to join them.

"There are quite a number of cables which appear to be obsolete, to ensure they are not in use or planned to be used, I want them taken down and put in the recycle bin." Eric just smiled. Lance looked at John.

"I will need your permission to go ahead John."

"Personally I think it is a good idea to get rid of the rubbish, which has accumulated over the years, so as far as I am concerned, remove it and I can appreciate your thinking Lance.

One thing you must bear in mind, some of the rooms have suspended ceilings, so some of the old cables might still be in the original roof cavity. Have fun."

John walked away chuckling.

"Dennis, before we start any other job shall we check the camera, just in case there has been any movement around the pin."

They went into a small room which had been kept locked and inspected the film from the camera covering the plastic pin but they were disappointed as there was no sign of any person or persons going near the clip.

Chapter 15

Dennis and Eric made a start shifting the old wiring out of the loft and putting it in the special bins which Lance had made available.

While working above the PM's office, Dennis could here a phone buzzing, he tried to peer through the ceiling tiles but it was not possible but he was still very puzzled.

When they came out of the loft, Dennis went in search of Lance, when he found him.

"May I speak to you privately sir?"

Lance took him by his arm and guided him into a small closet.

"What is bothering you Dennis?"

"When I was working above the PM's office, I could hear a buzzing sound."

"Right, shall we run the film back, we might be lucky?"

They sat winding the film back.

"Here we go Dennis" The film started running.

They both sat up with a jolt as they saw a young lady open a filing cabinet. She then looked around and picked up the phone and dialed a number, she spoke very briefly into the mouthpiece and then laid the phone on the desktop instead of placing the phone back on the cradle. After several minutes she replaced the phone and left the office. Lance rubbed his chin.

"I wonder."

They went into the office and Lance telephoned his office to speak to his secretary, then he rang off and he too laid the phone on the desk top. One minute passed the phone started to emit a loud buzzing tone. Lance and Dennis exchanged glances and Dennis nodded.

"That is the sound."

"It is a normal thing to happen, to remind a person that the phone has not been replaced correctly."

"That buzzing would have been long enough, for the receiver to be recalibrated to the same frequency as the transmitter. You are up against some very clever people sir."

*

Lance got out of his chair and turning to Dennis.

"Will you carry on working with Eric and I will speak to the PM and my boss but do not tell Eric of our suspicions."

Lance turned and left Dennis and went to speak the PM's aide.

"May I go into the PM's office as I want to speak to him privately?"

"Take a seat, I will ask him if it is convenient." Off he went.

He returned several minutes later.

"The PM will speak to you in five minutes time; he is just winding up a meeting."

Lance had just picked up a magazine to read when the PM walked into the room.

"Shall we go for a stroll in the garden Lance?"

They walked out of the back door into the large garden.

"Right Lance, any progress?"

"Yes sir. As you know Dennis altered the transmitting frequency of the plastic clip. Nothing has happened over the past ten days but today we saw one of your staff use the telephone and then left the phone off the hook, the buzzer started to attract one's attention that the phone was not correctly replaced. That buzzing was on long enough for the people at the other end to recalibrate their receiver. Incidentally, Dennis has altered the frequency again."

"Do you know which member of my staff was the culprit?"

"Yes sir, Is the lady who is in charge of your secretarial section to be trusted?"

"Absolutely Lance, She has been in this position for many years."

"Have I your permission to speak to her?"

"Certainly but I would like to know who the young lady is when you have spoken to Mrs. Christopher, agreed?"

"Better still sir; why not ask her to come to your main office, which is where I have the film set up."

"We will meet in my office in ten minutes time, okay?"

"Yes sir."

Lance sat down in the room; the PM's aide had put him before.

*

The young man walked into the room.

"The PM is ready for you now sir."

"Thank you, young man."

"Please follow me sir."

Lance entered the office and a tray containing a pot of coffee and biscuits were laid on the desk top.

"Lance, allow me to introduce you to Mrs. Christopher, she is in charge of all the secretary's in this building and I must add that she is completely trustworthy."

"Mrs. Christopher, I am delighted to meet you, after that build up I must watch my step."

This caused smiles all round. She got out of her chair and poured out the coffee, leaving Lance to add milk or sugar to his drink, naturally she knew how the PM likes his coffee.

They sat down to drink their coffee and the reason why she has been brought into the office was not mentioned. Having finished drinking their coffee, Lance set up the film for them to see.

"I would like to know the name of this young lady, Madam?"

"Her name is Tracy Green and she is a very efficient secretary, are you sure of what you are accusing her of?"

"Yes, I would say 99.9%"

"Good lord, I would never have thought it."

"I have taken you into our confidence, kindly respect me.

Please do not mention our conversation to any one but I'll advise you of any steps we might take."

Looking at the PM, he said.

"I must speak to my boss, Nathan, The Home Secretary before I speak to the girl."

He went into another room and phoned Nathan. When Nathan answered the phone Lance asked if he was free to join him urgently.

"Certainly Lance, from the tone of your voice I have no choice. Incidentally, I've trawled through the applications of all the secretarial staff and there are three people I would like to speak to. I'll be with you in one hour."

*

Nathan arrived and was greeted by Lance; he went right through the recent happenings.

"Lance, I am very impressed how quickly you have got to grips with this problem. Would you like me to be present when you interview this young lady?"

"Yes I would like both you and the PM present, one of you might spot something I might miss.

I have arranged for the interview to take place in the PM's office in ten minutes time, shall we go in?"

Tracy walked into the PM's office and Lance was very impressed. she was tall, slim with dark hair and eyes. Her figure was one which many ladies strive to achieve, either by exercising or going under the knife of a cosmetic surgeon.

Lance introduced himself to her and Nathan and of course you know the Prime Minister.

"Tracy, will you tell briefly your lifetime history?"

"I entered all my details on the confidential form which I signed. However, I will go through it again.

Both of my parents were killed in the same car accident when I was three years of age. An elderly aunt took me into her home and looked after me for about four years, I then went to a Masonic Girls Boarding School in Harrogate, I spent my holidays with my aunt in Derby, she is a wonderful person but she is now getting very frail.

I was very fortunate to gain a place at Cambridge University; I was financially supported by the Masons.

I graduated with an Honours Degree in the English language, which opened many doors for me.

My first position was as a Personnel Assistant to a Mr. Lee, company director with Marconi Communications Company. When a reshuffle took place Mr. Lee became a casualty, I was offered the same position with another director but I could not stand the man, he couldn't keep his hands to himself, I resigned.

I applied to the civil service, I was accepted and in view of my complete command of the English language I was offered an appointment here, which I accepted. That just about covers what you asked."

"Thank you Tracy for being so open and frank about your past but as you will appreciate the establishment must ensure every thing is correct for each person employed."

Tracy's eyes flashed.

"Don't you talk to me about the establishment; the so called establishment killed my grandfather."

Lance was taken aback.

"Why, do you say that Tracy?"

"My grandfather was killed in Switzerland by someone employed by the establishment, for why, neither my aunt, nor I know the reason?"

"What was his name Tracy?"

"He was a cosmetic surgeon named Robin Grenfell."

He heard a sudden sharp intake of breath; he looked round and realized it was Nathan.

"Our main concern is this; he switched on the film which had been set up.

Why did you place the phone on the desk top instead of putting it back on the pod, allowing the buzzing to start, after a few minutes you put it back on the cradle, why?"

"It was just a mistake, I use earpieces when I am typing letters which various ministers have put into their Dictaphones. It is that time of the day they all come rushing in to get their letters typed and they want them to go in the evening post.

In the film, you will see it is when I take the earpieces out of my ears, I realize the phone is buzzing, I then put it back on the pod."

"Why are you quizzing me sir, are you accusing me of doing something wrong?"

"Not at all Tracy, but we do have a leak from this office and we are carrying out a complete check of instruments and people." Lance smiled at her and she smiled back.

"Thank Tracy, you have been very cooperative and I appreciate your patience."

Tracy got out of her chair and left the room.

Nathan looked at Lance, "Well what do you think?"

The PM smiled.

"She is completely innocent or very clever."

Lance stood up and rubbed his chin.

"She struck me as being innocent but on the strength of our feelings do we let her stay here?"

He put the film on again and they watched it very carefully but they did not see anything different than previous viewings.

The PM stood up.

"There is nothing, we can sack or charge her with."

"I will send drinks in for you; I will have a word with the man who deals with filling vacancies in other departments."

Lance and Nathan sat enjoying their drinks, Lance turned round.

"What did you know about the death of Robin Grenfell, Nathan?

Your reaction made me jump."

"It must have been vigilantes Lance."

They smiled at each other.

The PM came back into the room.

"It has been suggested that Tracy should be promoted and fill a very senior position at the Smedley Hydro in Southport."

"That sounds a very satisfactory solution sir."

Lance looked up at the PM.

"May I suggest Dennis removes the plastic clip?"

"Yes Lance you do that and we will devise a way of tripping up the people who want to hear my conversations, but how?

Still, that is your department."

He walked away smiling.

Nathan and Lance left Downing Street and went back to their respective offices.

Chapter 16

Nathan arrived back at his office, as he sat down, his secretary came into his office carrying a cup of coffee, he smiled.

"Thank you. I can certainly do with that, life is getting so hectic these days, so many silly and unnecessary things happening."

He sat back enjoying the peace and quietness in his office, the phone ringing made him jump. As he picked up his phone, the caller said.

"Hello Nathan, this is Jan, I'm ringing to ensure that you will be able to attend a meeting in ten days time.

Bernie reckoned you were very busy, I thought I would check."

"How does he know I've had a problem?"

"Nathan, Bernie must have a fortune tellers crystal ball, he appears to know what is going on everywhere."

"Yes, there has been a problem; I will put you in the picture when we meet."

"Will you put the date I going to give you in your diary and I will confirm the venue at a later date. Hope you get your problem sorted and you will sleep better if you do."

Nathan called his secretary into his office and he started to clear the backlog of work that had built up while trying to solve the PM's leakage.

He asked his secretary to enter the date for the next meeting in his diary, he told her to enter it as a meeting with other government ministers to discuss the growing threat from terrorism, he smiled, when he thought of the vigilantes of which, he is taking part.

*

Nathan and Peter were advised of the venue for the meeting; again, it was to be held in the old castle in France. They decided they would go across on the ferry and hire a car rather than take their own cars, they felt it would be safer but they realized that they would still have to watch their backs.

They were the first to arrive, this gave Nathan an opportunity to explain the whole story how the bomb had been planted to explode, after the meeting in Hastings.

"My word, we were lucky Nathan, did you trace who was responsible?"

"No but we did trace the leakage in our PM's office. He asked the hotel to arrange accommodation for us all that night, the bomb was situated between the dining room and the bar and the hotel was devastated. The PM had gambled and it paid off. The real intention was for the explosion to take place during our meeting. The name Abdul Mohamed keeps coming up as a bomber."

Finally, the other four people had arrived and the chairman called the team into the office.

"Thank you for coming gentlemen, in the black bag there are just three names but I can tell you that these are the most vicious of the lot. Before we start, do you think two people should operate together in view of the men we are to eliminate this time?"

"We have two people from each country, how do you feel about each couple from the country they represent acting together?"

The German minister said.

"I think it is a good idea, it lessens the chance of a leakage in communication."

"Are you all agreed to work this way?"

They all nodded in agreement.

"There are three cards here, as before, one of the cards is the Ace of Spades, whoever picks up that card, will be the couple to deal with the elimination."

They all sat round the table; there was a sense of tension in the room. Jan stood up and dealt the three cards to the groups of two present, all three hesitantly picked up the card; Peter smiled at Nathan and showed him his card which was the Joker, Nathan felt very pleased, he didn't feel like having the responsibility of ending a person's life.

Picking up the small black bag, he asked the man sat next to him to take out a piece of paper with a name written on it.

The man pulled out the slip of paper and handed to Jan.

"Gentlemen, this is a tricky one, his name is Pierre Darlan."

"The dossier on this gentleman is that when France capitulated and signed the armistice with Germany, the Vichy Government came into being and Darlan was appointed as a senior officer in the secret police, which was called the Milice.

The secret police not only rounded up thousands of French Jews to be deported but they also concentrated on investigating the resistance groups and they acted like the Gestapo by using torture in an attempt to obtain information.

116

The group of Milice members not only tortured in an attempt to obtain information but they were sadist, many a Frenchman was left with broken bones and completely distorted and disfigured, it was never understood how they could treat their own countrymen in this manner.

These people became a great help to the Gestapo, they could deploy their troops elsewhere.

I've been advised that Klaus Gunter has identified me as the chairman of this group, I'll have to keep looking over my shoulder but this will not lessen my efforts to complete the task we all embarked on."

*

Henri Girard and his countryman Francoise Flowers met up to decide how to approach their duty of eliminating Pierre Darlan, it had been Henri who picked up the Ace of spades.

It was obvious that they could not use their previous ways of elimination, they will have to put their thinking caps on.

They agreed to meet up the following day and walk around the area, in which Darlan is living, hoping to get an inspiration.

When they approached Pierre's house they were shocked to see two men sitting in wheel chairs on the pavement outside the house, they looked just like two balls of flesh and bones and it was obvious that they would be unable to wear conventional clothing, they had a type of a cape covering their broken bodies.

Henri approached one of them;

"Pardon me monsieur, why are you sitting outside Pierre's house?"

"Why! He and his friends of the Milice broke every bone in my body trying to get me to betray my group of resistance fighters.

They laughed, when they finished breaking me they rolled me up as I am now. I am unable to move at all and I'm strapped in this chair by friends, who take care of my every need for not giving them away, which, would have resulted in them being killed. I am fed liquid food through a tube in my mouth and I operate this wheelchair with my mouthpiece, held in place by the clip around my head.

My pal Jon in the other chair was treated in the same way; I was displayed to other prisoners and told they would end up as I, if they did not cooperate. The days we are well enough, we sit here to shake his conscience, one day I will arrange to repay my debt to him."

"What is your name?"

"I am Paul and my friend is Jon."

"You may have found a friend, who will be able to help you to achieve the result you are aiming for."

"Paul, are your friends really trustworthy?"

"I guaranteed their lives, they will guarantee mine."

"Give me your address and I will call round one evening to discuss your objective."

Paul gave Henri his address.

"I don't know you but I trust you."

"Have no fear Paul you are speaking to a true Frenchman."

Francoise who had been standing nearby smiled at Henri as they walked away.

"We have found an ally and I feel quite confident that we will get some help."

"I get that impression too, Francoise."

Henri and Francoise, went back to Darlan's address several days later and found the two men still carrying on with their vigil, they arranged to visit their address that evening.

In the evening they went to the small village where Paul and Jon live, they found the house and Henri rang the door bell, the door was opened by a tall heavily built man.

"Who are you and what do you want?"

"Hello, Paul and Jon are expecting us."

"Yes, you must be Henri and Francoise," holding out his hand to shake.

"Do come in"

They were shown into a small room, there were six men sat around a table with Paul and Jon still in their wheelchairs, they were guided to the two vacant chairs.

The man sitting at the top of the table looked at them with a fixed grin on his face.

"Now tell me, what is the hope you have given to Paul and Jon, of punishing Darlan?"

"Whatever you say in this room will remain a complete secret. I am not foolish enough to threaten you, if you should betray us."

Henri looked straight at the man who had been speaking.

"We intend to kill him."

A deathly hush fell in the room for many seconds and the man started laughing and the others joined in.

"How do you plan to do that?"

"We don't know yet, that is why we were looking around Darlan's house trying to build up a picture of his habits and movements. That is how we met Jon and Paul."

"We are at the early planning stage; his death is to take place in such a way, that no one can be held responsible."

The head man looked at Henri and Francoise, smiling.

"Go away now and return in two or three days and we will discuss our and your plans and decide which plan contains the most plausible execution but deemed to be accidental."

"Have you carried out any surveillance of his daily movements yet?"

"No, Francoise tried to follow him but he is so well guarded and he made several car changes, he found it difficult.

Darlan must be on the jump, your two young men must be upsetting him."

"We want to know, what time he leaves home in the morning, does he drive or is he driven, where does he go for his lunch and from which vendor does he buy his paper? All these things are necessary to create a foolproof plan."

The man at the head of the table, still smiling, looked at Henri then Francoise and said.

"We will have a complete dossier ready for you in three days time, will that do?"

"We look forward to our next meeting."

*

Henri and Francoise spent time together trying to create a plan to eliminate Darlan but they did not succeed and they were most disappointed.

Several days later they met up and visited Jon and Paul's address. As the door opened, this time they were greeted with a hug and kissed on each cheek.

They went into the room; the man sat at the head of the table looked at them.

"Do sit down."

"Have you come up with a plan yet?"

"No, we have spent hours trying to create a suitable accident but without success."

"Here is the dossier we promised, when you read it, you will be surprised how thorough it is in detail.

His main hobby, come business, is breeding German shepherd dogs; he has large fenced runs in the garden behind the house."

"That's it." shouted Henri.

They all looked at him, stunned.

"Don't look so startled, if we could get one of his dogs to attack him with the Rabies infection."

The head man smiled.

"How will you arrange that?"

"At this stage I can't give you an answer."

"As most of you might know. Rabies is transmitted from the animal's saliva to an open wound, such as when a person or animal is bitten breaking the skin and the saliva enters the open wound. The virus travels along the victim's nerve fibres from the bite to the brain.

The face and the neck is the most affected part because these wounds need immediate attention. If the bite is on the lower limbs it would allow more time before treatment.

Symptoms, which appear when the virus has reached the brain, include muscle spasms, convulsions and extreme excitement and rage interrupted by periods of pain. If treated immediately after a bite, it is possible to prevent Rabies. However, once the disease is fully established in a person and they begin to show symptoms, it nearly always leads to death."

"That would be an ideal solution, if we could find a way how to administer the Rabies virus into Darlan's system. I doubt if one of his dogs would turn on him and in any case I would think his dogs will be clean."

"May I say something?"

They all looked at Jean.

"Darlan visits my cousins 'Coiffeur Pour Hommes' two or three times a week for a wet shave or hair trim. Is possible to work round that?"

"Brilliant Jean, do you think your cousin would join us in this venture?"

"His brother was shot by Darlan's troop of Milice; his group was ambushed while trying to derail a troop train headed for Normandy

In an attempt to push the invaders back, he hates Darlan just as much as we."

"It could work if during Darlan's wet shave the barber slightly nicks his chin.

Instead of using a septic pencil, a solution of saliva from a Rabies infective animal is used while Darlan thinks he is receiving treatment. We then hope he will not be aware of this until the symptoms take hold."

They all agreed on this plan, hoping the barber will cooperate.

*

Jean visited his cousin Jacque and explained to him about the meeting and how he could bring about the death of a member of the Milice. At first Jacque was a little hesitant but when Jean told him it was Darlan, he agreed immediately.

When Jean told him of the plan, Jacque agreed but the liquid supplied for him to use must not endanger him in any way.

"Yes Jacque that will be worked out before the liquid is delivered."

Jean went back to his friends and told them that Jacque will help.

Henri and Francoise went back that evening to Jon and Paul's address and they all sat down to discuss the plan.

"Where do we obtain the liquid?" not one of them could come up with the answer.

"I will contact a man who will know."

Henri telephoned Colonel Black's office the following morning; he was hoping that Bernie would be in the country at this time.

He was very fortunate; Bernie was in France on business and in his office, when Bernie picked up the phone, the caller said.

"May I speak to Colonel Black please?"

"Speaking, how can I help you?"

"Colonel Black, may we meet? I have a problem, which, I hope you may be able to help."

"From where are you phoning?"

Henri told him exactly where he was.

"Good, go to small coffee bar in the next street and I will join you in ten minutes."

Henri strolled round to the coffee bar; he ordered two coffees and sat down and a man came and sat down beside him.

"You are Henri?"

"Yes, you must be Colonel Black."

"Yes Henri but it is Bernie, are you comfortable with that?"

"Indeed I am."

"Now what is the problem, no, before we talk, I will order a cognac, will you join me?"

"Yes please, what a good idea."

"Now shall we get down to business?"

Henri proceeded to explain their plan to eliminate Darlan.

"Naturally, if you are unable or not prepared to help, please keep this information to yourself."

"Henri, it is a very good plan, we were going to deal with him ourselves. Several of my distant relatives were marched off to the concentration camps by the Milice, of which, this man was and possibly still is, a senior officer.

Meet me here the same time tomorrow and I will have what you need for your project."

Henri contacted Francoise and told him of his progress.

They met up with Bernie the following day as planned and he passed a sealed plastic bag to Henri.

"The virus is very potent and it looks like a septic pencil but when it is applied to the wound, squeeze the pencil, a liquid will infect the wound. If the victim is not treated in one hour or two at the latest, he will be dead in two days. A person using this pencil is quite safe, the outside of the pencil is treated and no liquid will escape."

A meeting was held at Jon and Paul's address, Jacque was invited to attend.

Henri passed the plastic bag to Jacque and he told him.

"It is in the form of a pencil but if you squeeze the pencil it will discharge a liquid to the wound, I am assured that the user is safe. When you have used it, place it back in the plastic bag and reseal it and take to Fred the blacksmith and he will put it in his furnace."

The morning Darlan went in for his shave, Jacque was feeling a little jumpy, however, Jacque went through the usual routine with the hot towels and then he spent time with the lather brush. Jacque had almost finished when he nicked Darlan's neck just below his left ear. He was very apologetic and proceeded to dab the cut with the septic pencil at the same time squeezing a small amount of liquid into the wound. Jacque powdered Darlan's face; Pierre paid and made another appointment for two days later, then left the shop.

Henri received a message from Bernie telling him that Pierre Darlan was quite ill; his own doctor thinks it is septicaemia but he is deteriorating and they are going to get the top Blood Specialist in the country to visit Pierre.

They hesitated, as the top man is Joseph Bloom and he is Jewish but they wanted the best for Pierre so the decided to ask Joseph to visit.

The specialist came along and carried out several tests but he was unable to save Pierre, he died two days later. He turned to the man in charge,

"I am sorry; there was little I could do for him."

"Pierre might meet my grand parents he ordered to be marched off to the concentration camp, where they were starved to death."

"You killed Pierre."

"Don't you dare accuse me of killing him, he died after contracting Rabies."

An inquest was held and the coroner confirmed that Pierre had died from Rabies and ordered all his dogs to be checked and kennels he visited recently.

*

That evening Henri and Francoise visited Jon and Paul, this time the long table was covered with bottles of wine and brandy. Jon and Paul were so excited and it was sad to see such happiness because of a man's death.

Henri and Francoise went to Pierre's funeral, they very surprised that there were no family member present, in fact, apart from Henri and Francoise there were only five mourners even the people he had worked with were not present.

The service took place in a small church within the burial grounds. They were told later that he had become such a vicious man, his wife and children left him and are living with her parents.

As the coffin was lowered into a deep grave, there was an explosion. This was followed by a cheer from group of ten men standing at the corner of the cemetery, all using walking sticks or on crutches.

Henri and Francoise shook hands and each went their own way. Henri undertook the task of entering Pierre's death in the Telegraph.

Chapter 17

Klaus received instructions to report to The Regent Berlin Hotel for a meeting with Frank von Kessler and Fritz Beckenbaugh, to discuss what, Klaus was not too sure.

As he entered the hotel a young man approached him.

"Are you Klaus Gunter sir?"

"Yes, I am "

"Follow me sir."

Klaus was guided along a long corridor to a door at the end of the corridor; he knocked on the door, a gruff voice called.

"Enter"

Klaus entered the room and recognized them straight away, he did not offer his hand to shake this time, he raised his right arm and gave the Nazi salute and the two men responded.

"Klaus Gunter, you have again failed to carry out the operation to eliminate Isaac Miller, he has returned to Germany in order his two sons can continue with their education."

"Through your negligence, the kidnapping of Isaac Millers two boys went horribly wrong and we, The Masters of the World were arrested and placed in a small disgusting prison cell like common criminals. Kidnapping in America carries the penalty of death. The only reason we were released is because we have a man in the Whitehouse on our payroll, we should have left you there.

Three of our special agents are being transferred to your team; we hope to hear a satisfactory result very soon.

"Klaus Gunter, this your last chance, if you foul this up again you will lose your money and perks."

*

Klaus was badly shaken, he had always been the man in charge and to be told that three agents would be put in his team was unsettling.

It would appear that he will have to plan to eliminate Isaac Miller, to keep the powerful members of the Nazi party happy.

Klaus has doubts in his own mind, if the party would ever again become a world power.

He would never voice his doubts aloud, if he did, he would be signing his own death warrant.

There are very influential industrialist, who firmly believe a new Fuehrer will arrive one day and bring about what Adolf Hitler strived to achieve.

Klaus called a meeting of his team and told them they would have three special agents joining them.

"He was really saddened to hear of the death of Pierre Darlan and it is necessary to track down his murderer and reap revenge.

I feel confident, if we can find the person or persons who planned the death of Pierre, it will lead us to the people responsible for the death of several of our friends.

Klaus organized two of his team to shadow Isaac Miller and submit a full dossier, from which, he can plan to eliminate him.

*

One of Bernie's team alerted him that Isaac was being shadowed.

"Not! Again."

Bernie visited the coffee bar where he had met Isaac before.

He found Isaac sat at his usual table, he looked up.

"Hello Bernie, I am delighted to meet you again."

"I am pleased to meet up with you Isaac, for some unknown reason you are being followed again. I thought they had given up on you but it is not the case.

I have instructed one of my team to apprehend one of the people who are following you and we will find out what is going on.

Isaac, just watch your back, be very careful and I will meet up with you next week."

Two of Bernie's team shadowed the man and at the end of the day when Isaac had been followed home, they pounced and bundled the man into a car. They took him back to Bernie's house come office to interrogate him but he refused answer any questions, they contacted Bernie.

"Don't use any physical violence or torture, put him in the small prison cell and deny him food and water until he is prepared to cooperate.

When he is ready to talk, contact me to join you."

Two days later, Bernie received a message saying the man was ready to talk.

He told Bernie that the dossier was for Klaus who is under pressure to kill Isaac Miller. Whoever it is above him, said it is his last chance, if he fails this time, he will be dismissed and he will lose his rank and his income. He will try his upmost to eliminate Isaac.

Bernie considered the situation very carefully; he decided to take an unprecedented step of visiting Klaus.

He contacted Klaus's office to obtain an appointment, as he walked into Klaus office, he looked up.

"What the hell do you want?"

"I just called, to tell you that it wasn't Isaac who killed Bill Funk. During the German occupation of France a young French boy watched Bill Funk march villagers, his mother, sisters and brothers into a church, locked all the doors and then set it on fire, murdering all the people inside the church. He swore, one day he would kill Bill Funk in revenge and he did. Unfortunately, he met with an accident on the Autobahn on his way back to France. I thought it was not an accident and perhaps you were involved."

"Get out of my office." Bernie looked at him.

"I have told you this, I thought it might get you off the hook, I regard you as a formable foe and I look forward our future battles."

"Get out."

Bernie left the building chuckling but he was still wondering what Klaus is up to.

Bernie made a point of visiting Isaac again and told him exactly what the man had told him how Klaus is under pressure to kill him.

Isaac told Bernie that he was going to report what he knew to the German police.

"Will they take your case seriously Isaac?"

"Yes, they are trying to bring all the Nazi threats to a halt and get the country to start working together as Germans; this country will then have a prosperous future."

Chapter 18

Jan von Krupp called a meeting which was to be held in a Paris hotel, Jan thought if they vary their venues it lessens the chances of being attacked as was planned at the Hastings Hotel.

When all the people were present he called the meeting to order.

"I must congratulate the people who carried the elimination of Pierre Darlan, he was very well protected but you still got under the radar screen to carry out your plan."

"Now gentlemen, before I start dealing out the cards, I have arranged a meal and drinks to be served in the next room, let's go and enjoy a first class meal."

Nathan and Peter were pleased, they had left home early in the day and they were not impressed with the food being served on the Ferry, they just had coffee.

They all agreed it was an excellent meal and the choice of wines to complement the food. When they had all eaten and enjoyed the coffee, several ordered a cognac.

They all left the dining room to return to the room Jan had reserved to hold the meeting. They all appeared a little merry from drinking the wine and the brandy and the room became a little boisterous.

Jan stood up.

"Now gentlemen, we come to the reason we are here."

He dealt the cards around the table and as expected the Ace of Spades fell to Nathan and Peter. Jan picked up a small black bag and asked the man next to him to select a slip of paper from the bag. He did and handed the paper to Jan. He looked at the piece of paper and smiled.

"The name of the next gentleman to be eliminated could prove to be extremely difficult. His name is Baron Braun; he has a large estate in Bavaria taking in parts of the Black Forrest.

He was present at the 1939 meeting in Düsseldorf but was considered too old to take an active part in the military, with which he did not agree.

He was given the position of organizing the distribution of food for all the concentration camps, through greed; he failed to carry out his duties of ensuring the humanity aid arrived at the camps.

He headed the organization, which, was trusted to deal with the distribution of the Red Cross Parcels but these were intercepted and the contents sold on the black market.

The prisoners were dependant on receiving these parcels, which, never did arrive and if any family member of the prisoner should send a parcel, that too was sold, the cigarettes were like pieces of gold to Braun's organization.

The so called trustees, who removed the bodies from the gas chamber, would trade some of the gold teeth and Jewels found hidden in the mouths of the women for cigarettes. The trustees were more than happy to trade for cigarettes and they would give up whatever Braun's team asked, in return for a cigar rather than take all the spoils to the camp commandant.

He became very rich at the expense of the prisoners lives, the death toll in the camps from starvation was unbelievable and unjust.

His hobbies are fishing and hunting the wild boar in his forest. I understand he employs staff to maintain his gardens, property and to wait on him inside his house, he lives like a lord."

Nathan and Peter exchanged glances, Peter shrugged his shoulders. Both were wondering how to approach the elimination of Baron Braun and they both felt a little uneasy in view of their senior position held within their own government.

*

Arriving back in London, Nathan called Lance Goodchild and Ken Lee to his office.

When all four were seated, Nathan said.

"We have a very difficult task to perform and as before, you must keep this conversation to yourselves. The man we are to eliminate is Baron Braun; have either of you heard of him?"

"Yes, he is well up the rich list, there have been many rumours as to how he accumulated such wealth. The last I heard was that he operated a Black Market during the German occupation of the European countries".

Peter then related how the Braun organization sold Red Cross parcels and parcels sent by families addressed to prisoners, the rotten devil.

"He has a large estate in Bavaria and a dense forest is on his land."

"The title of Baron has been passed down for centuries, he was not directly in line as he was a bastard son of the old Baron but as he was the only male sired by the old Baron, he was nominated to carry on the name of Baron Braun".

"Have either of you any suggestions who we should send to reconnoitre the lie of the land in the village next to the Barons estate?"

Lance and Ken sat looking at each other.

"Who do you think Ken?"

"Brian comes to mind and pair him with Roy Halsall who has recently returned from that area." Lance nodded in agreement.

Brian and Roy were called to Nathan's office where they were given all the details of their next project.

You have not worked together before, May I suggest you spend a couple of days talking and discussing the project and return with your decision if you are prepared to work with your new partner".

Several days later Brian and Roy returned to Nathan's office to say they could happily work together.

Nathan handed them a chit to obtain money from the cashier to cover their expenses.

They decided to fly to France and motor to a small village close to Baron Braun's estate. When they arrived in the village they were pleasantly surprised, there were two churches and two residential Inns.

They visited both Inns before deciding on which one to stay.

The name of the Inn of their choice was 'The Wild Boar' in view of the area it was aptly named. They had an excellent meal at their chosen Inn; after the meal they decided to stroll to the other Inn named 'The Pheasant' they found the beer excellent but much stronger than they have been used to.

It was very busy with people either just drinking or eating. One of the young ladies behind the bar was very chatty; she was showing off her knowledge of the English language.

She told them that most of the men of the village worked on the Baron Braun's estate or Baron Rothschild's, which is the larger of the two.

There was one gentleman sat by himself and he looked so miserable, Brian turned to the girl.

"Why does he look so miserable?"

"He has been unsociable for several years, there is a rumour that he blames Baron Braun for the death of his wife, whether that is true or not I can't say.

He speaks a little English; some say he was a prisoner of war held in England. What I am telling you is hearsay so don't make too much of it."

"What is his name?"

"He answers to the name of Franz."

Brian wandered over to the table where Franz was sitting.

"Hello Franz, did you spend much time in England?"

"Yes I did."

"Were you treated well?"

"O.K."

Brian realized it was going to be tough to strike up a conversation with Franz.

"Which part of the country were you?"

"I worked on a farm close to a place called Fleetwood," his broken English made it difficult to converse at first.

"You must have felt at home near the hills in the Lake District."

For the first time he smiled.

"Yes it was lovely countryside, much better to be there than being shot at by your Spitfires."

"Please don't take offence Franz but why do you look so miserable?"

"My lovely wife was killed and I find it difficult to live without her."

"I am so sorry, was it a road accident?"

"I don't wish to talk about it."

He drained glass, got out of his chair and left.

Both Brian and Roy felt they had made a little progress and they spent the next day wandering around the village, which, they found to be charming and the inhabitants friendly.

Roy suggested that they went to the Pheasant early hoping they would be in the bar when Franz came in. They were sure that it was from him they would be able to complete the dossier.

They were lucky, Roy was just at the bar paying for his beer when Franz walked in, Roy paid for his drink and invited him to join them, which he did.

The young lady behind the counter told them how surprised she was that Franz had sat and talked to them. I can't remember the last time I saw that happen.

Brian started asking him questions about Baron Braun's estate but he answers were very guarded.

"What are your duties on such a large estate when so many people are employed?"

This question appeared to open the door.

"I take care of the horses; the hunting dog and I clean and oil the Barons guns when he returns from a shoot.

He has one particular gun which he favours, this was presented to him when he retired from the army and it is beautiful. It was handmade with the stock decorated with the crest of his regiment inlaid with ivory.

He boasts that with his gun no wild boar can touch him."

"Is he a good man to work for?"

Franz fumbled over his words.

"I no answer that."

Roy looked at Brian and smiled.

Franz drained his tankard, bid them goodnight and left.

*

The following evening Brian decided they should try again to find out more about the estate from Franz.

When they walked into bar Franz was sat at the same table, Brian went to the bar to order their drinks, the young lady said.

"Please sit down, Franz ordered and paid for your drinks."

She put the tankards on the table, they both said.

"Thank you, cheers" and Franz really smiled for the first time.

The young lady standing behind the bar, smiled.

They sat chatting about the weather and they told him how impressed they were with the village.

He just smiled; "It is a wonderful village."

"Irma and I walked around the village every evening."

"Have you any family Franz?"

"No, I am sorry to say, we both were hoping for a son but it was not to be."

"I am sorry to hear of your disappointment."

"Last night you asked me about Baron Braun, he is a vile man.

He tried to rape my wife in the wine cellar and she managed to push him away as two staff members came down the cellar steps. Had they not come down he would have raped my wife, without any witness, his word would have been accepted against the word of my wife. When she told me, I wanted to shoot him but my wife persuaded me not to take any action as we had no where else to live."

"I am convinced! This is what happened when Irma was working in the attic. He was seen going to the attic and he went with the express purpose of raping her.

When he attacked her she would have pushed him away and rushed through the open door and slipped and fell, her body hit several buttresses on the way down, she would have been dead before she landed on the ground"

"That is a very sad story."

"I swore that I would kill the Baron after the funeral, I still try to plan how it will happen one day, when I can work out a plan to achieve his death without implicating myself and remain blameless.

I should not have told you my story, please keep it to yourselves?"

"Of course we will Franz, perhaps we can help you, I don't know in what way yet. We will think about it and meet you tomorrow evening. Have no fear Franz; your secret is safe with us."

*

Two evenings later they went to the Pheasant Inn and found Franz sat at his usual table, they bought their beer and went to sit with him.

He looked at them.

"Had any thoughts?"

"Not concrete."

"I might be late tomorrow evening, a group of wild boars have been spotted in the forest and that is the Baron's sport.

In the morning he will want to be out early and he will go alone in his pickup truck with his dog in the back and will park on the outskirts of the forest.

The pattern is always the same, he and the dog will track the boars, he will shoot one and I or someone else will be told to go into the forest and collect the dead boar and take it to the cook.

I will clean and oil his favourite gun early in the morning, ready for him to take with him." Roy looked at him and smiled.

"Have you never thought of removing the firing pin?"

"Good lord, no, I haven't but it would be very easy thing to do, touching the side of his nose with a finger."

*

Franz was up very early the following morning to take care of feeding the Barons hunting dog, when he had fed the dog, he then took the Baron's favourite rifle from the firearms rack and proceeded to clean and oil the rifle to ensure it was in working order. He then took a leather bandolier from the cupboard and slotted the bullets in the loops.

Thinking about the firing pin Roy had spoken about, he looked, there was just one small screw holding the pin in position. He made a quick decision, he unscrewed the small screw and removed the pin and replaced the screw and it was not obvious to the eye that the pin had been removed. He put the small screwdriver and the pin in his pocket.

*

The Baron came striding into the outhouse, the dog nuzzled up to him to be fondled but he raised his foot and kicked the dog away.

"Franz, arrange a party to collect the boar when I come back and I will enjoy it for my dinner."

He picked up his gun and bandolier and jumped into the pickup, the dog jumped in the back and off he went.

The Baron kept to his normal pattern, he parked just outside the forest, he, left the pickup and strode off.

When he arrived in the dense part of the forest, his dog started barking and jumping about.

He suddenly spotted two adult boars and a family of four.

The sun was just rising and the tusks of the large male boar glistened in the sunlight.

The boar looked up and started to advance towards the Baron and it started scraping the ground with its front right hoof as a bull would do facing a matador in the Bull Ring.

He checked that he had a bullet in the chamber of the rifle. He spoke to the animal, come closer fatty; I will shoot you right between your eyes and you will be my supper. Baron put his gun to his shoulder waiting for the boar to move closer, he aimed and pulled the trigger, nothing happened, the gun did not fire.

The boar lunged at him knocking him to the ground and the tusks ripped his belly open. The dog tried to protect its master but it was no match against the tusks and the dog lay dying.

The boar again turned its attention to the Baron and it repeatedly ripped his flesh with his tusks.

Looking at the clock, Franz realized the Baron should have returned by now, he decided to investigate. He went into the forest and he found the body of the Baron and his dog, both bodies had been partially eaten by the boar family.

Franz quickly replaced the pin and then drove the pickup back to the house to raise the alarm. Nobody could understand how it could have happened; the rifle had not been fired.

The authorities were quickly on the scene.

One of the first things they asked for was the rifle, which would be taken away for examination.

Franz was quite comfortable about handing over the gun.

The fact the pin had been removed and then replaced could not be identified as a fault, the screw holding the pin has a film of oil covering it.

Franz was interviewed, the question asked was.

"At what time did the Baron leave this morning in the pickup? They were surprised that he had not fired the gun.

The only answer they could come up with was the wild boar had taken him by surprise, flooring him before he could raise his rifle.

It was referred to as a terrible accident and the police and the medical team left, leaving the undertaker to take the Barons body to the coroner's mortuary for examination.

*

Franz did go to the Pheasant Inn but much later than his normal time, the young girl in the bar remarked.

"You are late this evening, everything okay?"

"No, we had a terrible tragedy at the hall. The Baron was attacked by a wild boar and it killed him."

He collected his beer and went to his usual table. He was sitting down as Brian and Roy walked in the bar, they bought the drinks and went and joined Franz.

"We have had a terrible tragedy; the Baron was attacked and killed by a wild boar."

"What a terrible thing to happen, I thought he said he could deal with any animal."

"This one must have taken him by surprise because he did not have time to shoot it."

There was a slight smile on his lips.

"The authorities came and questioned me and the others who went with me to witness the dead body in the forest. They inspected the rifle and could not find any fault, the bullet was in the chamber to be fired and they fired it to ensure there was not a malfunction. It will be up to the coroner to decide the cause of Baron Braun's death."

They met up with Franz the following evening and told him they were returning to England the following day. Brian gave Franz his home address and invited him to visit any time. They thanked the staff of the Inn for making their stay so pleasant.

They flew back to England the following day and arrived in London about lunchtime. They made their way to Nathan's office and asked his secretary if they could speak to him, she went into his office, Nathan came straight out.

"Do come in, Peter is here."

They told them that the Baron had met his death at the tusks of a wild boar. They both smiled.

"Peter and I are most grateful; you have done really well on the assignment. We will ensure our gratitude is reflected in your bonus."

As they left, Nathan contacted the Telegraph Newspaper to insert a message in the obituary column.

Outside, Brian turned to Roy, "Come along I'm buying the beer."

Chapter 19

A few months later Nathan and Peter were notified of another meeting and they were both having some reservations about being a vigilante. Nathan's main purpose in his job is to safeguard his country against terrorist and here he was doing just the opposite.

The venue for the meeting was again to be held in an old castle in the south of France, they decided to fly and then hire a car and this would break up the journey.

When they arrived, they were greeted by Jan and he told them to go to the reception desk as he had booked them in for an overnight stay. They signed the register and were given the keys to a twin bedded room, which suited both Nathan and Peter.

When Peter opened the bedroom door, he was amazed, it had a very comfortable lounge area and it was an elegant apartment. Nathan dropped into a large armchair.

"This will do Peter."

They showered and then went into the lift to go downstairs to the dining room. The people present were those they had met on previous occasions, although there was a language barrier, they each made themselves understood.

Jan came into the room.

*

"Gentlemen, before we eat will you all kindly join me in the other room as I've some information I wish to pass on."

They all followed Jan into the reserved room and sat around a table.

"Several months ago, I told you we had traced the paymaster for the Nazi Officers but couldn't do anything to stop it. The Swiss government decided to investigate how all the individual accounts were transferred to a charity called "Officers Charity". In this charity, there is still a mountain of cash but no records are available to trace from which accounts the cash originated. All the records have been destroyed or stolen; it is obvious some one had been paid to take care of the destruction of the records.

The Swiss government took the case to the law high courts but nothing could be done to halt the monthly payments, the judges ruled that the money from the individual accounts will have been donated, not stolen.

One wonders how much money changed hands for the judges to arrive at this decision.

One other thing I must tell you. You will remember I told you I was called to Berlin and told to trace the vigilantes; I was phoned asking me to make a report on my progress. I told them I was on a special assignment, I got a friend of mine who is a senior officer to confirm this and he did. So at present I am off the hook."

*

"Before we go back into the dining room to eat, I will deal with question of elimination."

"I must say, how surprised I was to read of Baron Braun's death. I was convinced it would be a very long and difficult assignment, so congratulations to whoever dealt with it."

Jan picked up a small pile of playing cards and dealt out three cards, Nathan looking round guessed by the look on Isaac's face, it was he who had the Ace of Spades. Isaac's partner is Boris Bormann.

Jan offered the black bag to the man sat next to him, the man pulled out the one remaining slip of paper and handed it to Jan...

"The next gentleman to receive our attention is Herman Brant."

"This gentleman was charged with murder, rape, theft and inhumane treatment meted out to the slave labourers. He was to be tried in Nuremberg but he slipped the net and he lives a normal life in Hanover. How he and others got away with the terrible atrocities they committed, we shall never know.

He was in charge of large Steel and Iron Foundry plus an adjoining ammunition factory. The bulk of his workforce was slave labour transported from the occupied countries. The qualified engineers and the scientists in charge were people who were regarded as collaborators and were secretly despised by the slave workers.

The furnaces on site were capable of melting iron ore to be poured into moulds necessary to produce rifles or heavy artillery guns.

When he received a consignment of slave labour, he would inspect them on arrival. If he saw any attractive young ladies among the newcomers he would put them in the office to work and they would last in that job for about two weeks, then they would be put on the shop floor, working long hours each day as opposed to the 6 hours each day in the office.

The workmen realized what was happening but they were helpless to intervene.

He would make the slave labour work for 18 hours each day and if they were caught slacking, they would either be given an extra hour to work or a cut in their food ration and this was a real punishment, as the full food ration was very meager.

If any of the workers should be accused of being an agitator and causing unrest with the other workers, he would disappear over night, the following day there would be another man doing his job. It was rumoured that the large furnace was their last resting place.

There were several attempts on the life of Herman but they were unsuccessful.

He lives in Hanover and he spends a lot of his time with his hobbies, which are Golf and Archery, he has no wife or family, they all left him five years ago.

*

Isaac and Boris planned a meeting to discuss the elimination of Herman Brant.

Isaac did wonder how Boris would react to working with a Jew, to eliminate a German. When they did meet up, there was no sign of any animosity from Boris.

They started discussing how they should approach their project; they discussed how they could plan Herman's death. His death could be on the Archery field but his death would be placed at the door of a person, which, they did not want.

They decided it would have to be an accident on the road or on the golf course. They both agreed to meet again in two days time, hoping that one of them had come up with a foolproof plan.

When they did meet up again, Boris had come up with a plan.

His plan is, get several world war two old hand grenades to detonate in such a way to kill Herman.

Isaac smiled,

"May I suggest we try to get two or three old rusty hand grenades, put them in one of the small copse nearest to the clubhouse and explode one?

The people will run out of the clubhouse to investigate the explosion, they will find another two grenades in the undergrowth; they will contact the bomb squad to deal with them. They will also carry out a search to ensure there were no more in the copse.

At a later date we get another two or three hand grenades and perhaps a primed shell ready to strike at Herman. We must decide which one of the several copses we will use, this we can decide by watching Herman when he goes round the golf course by himself practicing."

"Where do we get these items from Isaac?"

"I might be able to find a source, if I am unable to do so, I will contact you, hoping you have found a supplier."

*

The first man Isaac thought of was Colonel Black; he left a message at several places hoping he will make contact.

The following day he went to his usual coffee bar, hoping Bernie will join him but he was disappointed.

However, during the evening he received a phone call, the man on the line said.

"I will meet you for coffee tomorrow morning" and Isaac heard the receiver being replaced on the cradle, he smiled, obviously Bernie did not want to prolong the conversation.

Bernie did meet Isaac at the coffee bar and as before they enjoyed a cognac with their coffee.

"Now, Isaac, how can I help you?"

Isaac outlined their plan. Bernie smiled.

"I like how you plan to have an explosion near the clubhouse and the old hand grenades found when the explosion is investigated."

"You are asking me where you might get the old and rusty grenades."

"The second explosion should be with a primed shell, which will give you the desired affect and of course you will have to put several grenades in the undergrowth for when the investigation takes place.

Have you decided how you will ignite the shell?"

"No, we have not worked that one out yet."

"The first explosion close to the clubhouse, the grenade can be thrown but not the second explosion for the planned elimination, this must be planned carefully."

"I will leave a box containing the items you want at your office in the warehouse in a couple of days. The primers will be in the box wrapped in cellophane.

You do know how to remove the screw at the base of the grenade and slip the primer inside?"

"Yes, I have done it before?"

"The two shells will be primed but you will have to decide on how to detonate one of them for the second explosion."

Isaac thanked Bernie, he got out of his chair and left, Isaac then contacted Boris and arranged to meet.

Isaac was at the café first so he ordered the coffee; Boris arrived just as the waiter placed the cups on the table. Boris smiled.

"How's that for timing?"

*

Boris and Isaac discussed the plan and they decided to explode one of the grenades in the copse, nearest to the clubhouse as previously discussed and leaving another grenade to be found in the undergrowth.

The evening was decided on, it was the following Friday, which is the night the annual dinner and dance was being held at the club.

It was decided that they would throw a grenade from the far side of the copse and quickly go round to the back of the club and join the crowd, who they hoped, would rush out of the clubhouse to investigate the explosion.

Friday evening they met up and went into a bar for a drink, waiting for darkness to close in. They finished their drinks and set off walking to the rear of the golf course.

It was quite a lavish affair, the ladies dressed in their finery and displaying their jewellery and of course all the men were in their dress suits.

Boris threw an old rusty grenade into the undergrowth and walked quite a way from the copse.

They could see through the windows of the club, the waiters were moving around serving the tables; they waited until the party people had finished their meal but before the dance band struck up, they decided to strike.

*

Isaac put his finger in the ring and pulled out the pin holding the primer, he counted one, two and threw the grenade into the copse and they ran round to the back of the clubhouse, hoping to mingle with the people coming out of the dining area to investigate the explosion..

Boris and Isaac began to get a little uneasy, the bomb should have activated by now, suddenly it exploded and it echoed making a terrific loud bang.

As they had hoped, the people rushed out of the dining room of the clubhouse.

The people were held back from where the explosion had taken place, the police had been sent for and on arrival the police searched the copse and found another grenade lying in the undergrowth.

They immediately sent for the bomb disposal squad and when the specialists arrived wearing protected clothing, they picked up the old rusty grenade that had been found and took it away, the people gathered round, gave them a cheer and hand clapping as the specialists were driven away.

Rumours were rife running round the crowd, until, one of the police said the grenade had been hidden in the undergrowth for many years, perhaps from World War 2; the copse will be searched thoroughly tomorrow in the daylight. One man said.

"Thank goodness I wasn't on the green."

Boris and Isaac walked away very satisfied, the first part of their operation had gone smoothly.

*

Several days later Isaac was sitting at a table of a pavement café, a voice said.

"Hello Isaac" he lowered his newspaper and looked up.

"Hello Bernie, coffee?"

"Yes please. Have you read page four Isaac?"

"No, not yet."

"Do read it; there is a write up about hand grenades that have been found on the local golf course, one of which exploded last week-end causing an upset at the annual club dinner."

"Have you decided how you are going to ignite one of the primed shells?"

"No, we hope to get some help on how to ignite the shell"

Bernie had a small plastic bang in his hand.

"Right, here is a small amount of plastic explosive and a detonator, stick the plastic to the base of the shell on the firing pin, stick the pencil shaped pin into the plastic but leave the round red top sticking out"

Bernie passed him another bag.

"When you press the key on this monitor it will explode the plastic explosive and this in turn will explode the shell, you will find it will devastate a wide area."

"Are you okay with that Isaac or shall I go through it again?" said Bernie smiling.

"Thank you Bernie, you will know if I have connected it wrongly by reading the obituary column."

"At what distance will the monitor activate the plastic explosive?"

"I would say 200 yards, far enough to keep you out of trouble."

Boris and Isaac were very careful not to been seen but they set up a watch on Herman's practice days and one thing, which came to light was, he sits on a form when he reaches the ninth hole.

His routine is to sit down and take a drink from his hip flask and then light a cigarette, when he had finished smoking his cigarette, he tees up a ball and carries on playing.

His practice days are Tuesday and Thursday and he starts his practice very early, in fact, at that time of the morning he is the only person on the course.

*

They agreed to put the primed shell near the seat and the other shell and the hand grenades in the undergrowth of the copses at the ninth hole on Monday night, ready for Herman's practice round in the following morning.

Sadie, Isaac's wife kept asking him what was bothering him? Although he said nothing was bothering him but Sadie knew differently, she had been married to Isaac too long to know when he was worried.

They were both out early on Tuesday morning but there was no Herman at seven o'clock, which was his usual time.

"Have we got it wrong Isaac?"

"I don't think so"

They saw a figure driving off the first green.

They positioned themselves on the far side of the copse away from the seat and waited, hoping it was Herman and that he would follow his normal routine.

Herman approached the green, he stood for a while and both Boris and Isaac were mentally willing him to sit down.

Herman did sit down and pulled out his hip flask and put it to his lips to drink.

Isaac pressed the button on the monitor, ten seconds later there was an almighty explosion they were blown off their feet.

They waited until several people were running towards the green before they ventured out of the copse to see if they had achieved their objective, they had but Isaac felt very guilty for taking a life.

A police car came speeding across the course, looking around they discovered a primed shell and two hand grenades.

Boris and Isaac drifted away and went to a café bar and enjoyed a coffee and cognac.

"I will deal with Telegraph Newspaper announcement Isaac" and they parted company.

During the evening, the door bell rang. Isaac went to the front door, when he opened the door he found two policemen on the doorstep.

"Are you Herr Miller?"

"Yes I am how can I help you?"

"You complained about being followed, we arrested the man who was following you and we found out that he is employed by Klaus Gunter. We interviewed Herr Gunter and he was told, if you are harmed in any way he will be held responsible.

"Thank you for coming and putting my mind at rest."

"Good night sir."

Isaac sat down in a chair, WOOSH!! he wondered what they wanted.

Several days later an inquiry was held and the coroner had the golf course closed while the Army sent their bomb disposal teams to scour every inch of the course and report when it was all clear.

The officer in charge was called to the stand and was subjected to an hour of questioning. For some reason the coroner called several army personnel to the stand before deliberating his verdict.

The coroner's verdict was that it had been a tragic accident caused by the explosion of an old wartime bomb.

Chapter 20

Bill Funk's wife Bella, finally came to terms with the death of her husband. She decided to organize an annual dinner for the wives of Nazi Officers as had been the practice in the past.

When she suggested it to some of the other ladies, the response was spontaneous.

"Let's do it."

Gradually the numbers interested mushroomed to such an extent, it was decided a social committee should be formed to deal with the project.

Two of Bella's friends, Bertha Spiers and Helga Schelling offered themselves to become committee members and it was only then, that Bella learned that their husbands had also died in a serious tragic accident and they had moved back to live in Germany.

How could this happen, she thought?

Bella was staggered by the number of wives applying to join, they decided to arrange a luncheon and explore the possibilities of arranging the function at the Regal Hotel Berlin and this is the only hotel capable of providing the service they would require.

The luncheon was a great success; it was decided to meet up again in one month's time to finalize the planned function. The ladies were so excited; this is the first time they have been able to get together, as they did in the past. Several had lost their husbands and such a meeting they found it to be a great help. Every one is eagerly looking forward to the dinner and hoping that they can find a suitable after dinner speaker.

*

Bella contacted friends and they suggested a senior government member who is quite used to speaking. She telephoned the gentleman and he agreed to be the after dinner speaker.

The evening was such a success that the ladies want a repeat rather than wait for another year to pass. They agreed to support another dinner as soon as it could be organized.

Several of the ladies sat round talking.

Helga suddenly said.

"Why has my money ceased to arrive since my husband died? Any idea?"

"Mine failed to arrive, I contacted Klaus Gunter and he arranged for the money to arrive again." said, Bertha Spiers.

"Right, I must speak to Klaus myself, I was given to understand that the "Officers Charity" was to support the officers during their lifetime and at the time of their death, the payment would automatically be transferred to his wife and family."

Helga contacted Klaus asking for an appointment for her and two friends to discuss a problem that is worrying all three of them.

Klaus contacted Helga by return, inviting all three of the ladies to visit him in his office and suggested a date and time.

They went along to his office, on arrival he had coffee organized and they sat down to enjoy their drinks.

"Now then ladies, how is it you think I can help you?"

They each looked at Helga.

"Some of the ladies are receiving monthly payments from The Officers Charity and some are not, why?"

"I am unable to give you the answer to your question but I will find out. Helga, how did your husband die?"

"His fishing boat hit a mine which killed him and his old friend."

"Did you honestly think it was an accident?"

"Yes, I was told by the authorities and I believed them, why shouldn't I?"

"Bella, how did your Bill die?"

"He was drunk and went to sleep and the fumes from an air freshener killed him, the wrong container was packed in error at the warehouse."

"Now I will ask you, was it a genuine accident?"

"Of course, that was the verdict of the enquiry."

"I will ask you he same question Bertha, how did Otto die?"

"He died because the air tanks were insufficiently topped up to supply enough oxygen when he went deep"

"Do you honestly believe that Otto would go deep unprepared?"

"That was what I was told by his minders and it was the coroners verdict, what else am I to think?"

"I will tell you what I think;

I think your husbands were murdered because they failed to stand trial in Nuremberg by leaving the country and a team of vigilantes have been carrying out these murders.

The next time you ladies get together, find out if any of the others lost their husbands through a tragic accident. I think you will find they did but I would like to know."

They promised keep him advised of their progress.

*

They left Klaus's office a little perplexed; all three were upset to think their husband's death was not as they thought,

Helga said.

"The first thing we will look in to, did our husband's die at the hands of the vigilantes and how many of our ladies are going to think the same as we three."

They had the names and addresses of the ladies who attended the dinner and they decided split the list into three and each one would

investigate how many had lost their husband's through a tragic accident.

When they met ten day's later, they were surprised by the number.

They contacted Klaus, he immediately arranged a meeting.

He too, was very surprised to be told the number of deaths attributed to tragic accidents was nine.

"Would your ladies be prepared to join in an investigation as to how these accidents occurred and the most important thing of all, who was responsible?"

Helga being the spokesperson said.

"Yes, I am sure they would all welcome the chance to join the group but three ladies who will be unable to take part, their health will not allow them the necessary flexibility, physically or mentally, that leaves six people you can count on. In view of our findings, the other three may insist on taking part.

"Most of the ladies were members of the Nazi Ladies Youth Army, so we are well trained in the art of self defense, shooting and dealing with explosives. You can see we are a force to be reckoned with."

"Good. Leave it with me; give your phone numbers to my secretary."

*

Helga and Bella decided to investigate the nearest address to them, which was the death of Baron Braun in Bavaria. Checking the address they found that Baroness Braun was living just outside Berlin and she had been there for a number of years. She and her husband had split up and she had brought the children to live with her parents.

Helga telephoned Giselle to make an appointment to visit; she was delighted to have their visit to look forward to. When they arrived, Giselle made them very welcome.

As they sat, drinking coffee. Helga said,

"Do you think your husband's death was a tragic accident?"

"Yes, on many occasion he would say how he had teased the male boar and waited until the animal lunged at him and he would shoot it between the eyes and it would slump to the floor dead. I expected him to meet his death in this manner long before now so I don't think it was murder"

"So you have no doubt about the way he died?"

"None, whatsoever."

"The reason we came to ask you was because Klaus Gunter is not completely convinced how some of the Ex Nazi Officers have died recently. Incidentally, are you receiving your monthly payments?"

"What payments?"

"The Baron would have been receiving monthly payments and now it should be paid to you since his death. I will tell Klaus that you are not in receipt of the payment and he will deal with it."

They said their good byes and left Giselle telling her that they will contact her when the plans are finalized for the next luncheon.

Several days later they visited Klaus and told him that Giselle had expected a boar to kill the Baron long before now and asked him to deal with her monthly payments.

*

Klaus asked if she would arrange to visit Gen Bruno Rossi's wife, Juliet and ask the same question about her husband's death. I will arrange the cash to be made available to you to cover your travel and hotel expenses. Helga and Bella made the necessary plans to visit Juliet and she was delighted when they arrived.

When they were sat enjoying a glass of wine, Helga turned to Juliet saying.

"What are your feelings over the accidental death of your husband?"

"They told me it was a genuine accident, why do you ask?"

"Nine of the ladies have lost their husbands through tragic accidents but the authorities are convinced they have been murdered, they were not accidental deaths."

"I will show you his motorcycle; it is in the garage, his friend who is an engineer did not agree with the coroner's summary or the verdict. The oil plug on the gearbox was replaced at the last oil change and a solution of lock tight was added to the threads and it would have needed a spanner to loosen the nut."

Helga asked Juliet where she could find the engineer and what is his name?

"Roberto Nevello and you will find him in the car showrooms hundred yards down the road."

Helga and Bella told Juliet they would call before they left to return home after speaking to Roberto.

"No. Let me go with you."

"Okay, you can show us Roberto's garage."

Arriving at the garage, Juliet pointed out Roberto, he looked up.

"Hello, Juliet, how can I help you?"

"My friends are of the same opinion as you; the gearbox oil plug must have been tampered with on Bruno's motorcycle."

"That is my opinion but I cannot prove it."

Helga turned to him.

"If you were looking for an engineer to carry out such a deed for money, who would you think of?"

"Only one man that comes to mind and that isTomo, he is a shady character; he would sell his grand parents for money."

"Where can he be found?"

"Go straight down this road until you come to a piece of waste ground and it is full of rusty cars, lorries and coaches that is Tomo's place. Please don't mention my name."

They set off and went down the road and they spotted the waste ground, which Roberto had mentioned. They walked round to the front of the garage and they were approached by a small dirty, unkempt individual.

"Can I help you?"

"Yes. You can, was it you who attended to Bruno's motorcycle before the accident?"

"No, why do you ask?"

"We were told that you were paid to attend to a little job?"

"What if I did?"

"Who paid you to loosen the gearbox oil plug?"

"Now then, I did no such thing."

"You did Tomo and I want to know who paid you. I am determined to get the name, you have no where to hide. I must tell you, my friends and I worked for the Gestapo during the war our job was to interrogate prisoners connected to any resistant group. It was an unpleasant job but we got results.

I think it's only fair that you should know who you are dealing with. You will tell me what I want to know eventually."

"I'm telling you, I had nothing to do with Bruno's motorcycle."

"I'm telling you Tomo, that you accepted money to loosen the gearbox plug on Bruno's motorcycle. I only want to know who paid you, just give me his name and I will not speak to you about this again or mention it to anyone else, you have my word."

"Right. The only name I heard mentioned was Henri, a small bearded Frenchman. He offered me a large amount of money, I pocketed the money but I didn't do the job, a young engineer who had a grudge against Bruno carried out the work and they thought I did the job.

I couldn't turn the job down but I didn't realize why he wanted the adjustment carried out. I thought it was to be a practical joke, not to kill a man. I do illegal jobs as selling on stolen cars but not where a person's life is at stake, on this, I give you my word."

"Will you call back later, give me a couple of hours and I will ask around?"

"Thanks Tomo, I will call later"

"So far, so good."

"Why not come back to my house and I will rustle up a light meal?"

"Thanks Juliet, you are kind."

"Not at all, you are my friends."

"After the meal, they sat around chatting."

Helga jumped up out of her chair.

"Shall we go?"

When they arrived at Tomo's garage, he handed Helga a piece of paper and written on it was the name Henri DuPont.

"Thank you Tomo, shaking his hand. I don't think we shall meet again" said Helga smiling.

When they arrived back home, Helga phoned Klaus and arranged to visit the following day.

Helga and Bella both went to Klaus's office the following morning, as they entered, Klaus stood up.

"Well?"

"The man who paid to have the oil plug loosened was a small bearded Frenchman named Henri DuPont."

"Good work, I will locate him and keep you informed.

*

Several weeks later Helga received a message from Klaus asking her to visit. As she entered his office he stood up saying.

"Hello Helga, we have traced Henri DuPont to a small village on the French and German border, the name of the village is yet to be confirmed but one of my men will trace him now we know his approximate location."

As they were talking the telephone started to ring,

Klaus picked up the receiver and Helga could hear a man speaking, Klaus said.

"Good god, when did this happen?"

"Two days ago, strange isn't it?"

He turned to Helga.

"Henri was driving his mini bus along a mountain road, when a lorry came along side and pushed him into a ravine, as it left the road it exploded.

The explosion was so powerful that neither the mini bus or Henri was identifiable, they found a number plate belonging to the vehicle."

Klaus looked at Helga with his penetrating eyes, she was smiling, a smile which he recognized.

"Helga, we won't speak about it any more."

*

Jan was alerted by Bernie. The people who eliminated the Ex Nazi Officers who were on the list compiled in Dusseldorf in 1939 are now being targeted.

Henri had been traced but by whom, Jan was not sure but Henri had paid the price by his life.

Jan was devastated when he first heard the news of Henri's death.

"The Hunters are now the Hunted."

He contacted the remaining people and suggested a meeting in one month's time. He thought if he left it one month, things will have settled down after Henri's death and they would feel much more comfortable.

Jan had not reckoned on the mole in his office, feeding Helga and her small army of widows with all the information.

*

Helga called a meeting of her ladies; several had agreed to join Bella, Bertha and Helga. The new recruits were Greta Ingle, Heidi Grenfell and Juliet Rossi. They all sat down in the reserved room in a hotel, which was a reasonable distance from each of their homes, Helga smiled when then took their coats off and saw they were wearing brown shirts.

Bertha Speirs has now moved from Brazil to Berlin, to join in the ladies venture to get revenge, much against her wealthy parent's wishes. As you know, the man who was responsible for Juliet's husband's death died last week in an accident. They all smiled and toasted Juliet.

Helga looked around;

"I have received information that my husband was killed on the orders of an English MP Peter Horn.

One of his agents who were caught messing with Alfred's fishing boat, doing something with the gas supply, he was caught and dealt with but Alfred's boat still exploded and killed him and his friend.

They said it was an old war time mine but it wasn't, it was the calor gas in the bilges. Now ladies, he is our next target.

Go around and see if you can find out any information about Peter Horn's weak spots and report back here in two weeks time."

*

Two weeks later, they all met up in the same hotel as arranged and they had very little to report on Peter Horn. As an MP he is chauffeured to his office or Westminster and to his home and he has a bodyguard who is invisible, but he is there.

"He will be attending a meeting in two weeks time and he will be travelling with Britain's Home Secretary, Nathan Garland. MP and he must be involved in some way. I suggest we try and find out to what extent he was involved; if he was, we can deal with both at the same time."

"That is good thinking Bertha."

"You are right Bertha, I received information that Nathan was responsible for the death of your husband, Otto Spiers, he sent two of his agents to Brazil to complete a dossier on his movements. Nathan's agents were somehow sidelined and they received a lot of help from the Zionist secret service, the man in charge was a Colonel Black and Otto died before Nathan's agents returned home but I still think Nathan was responsible. It goes to prove that if he is going to attend a meeting called by Jan Von Krupp, he must have been involved in the elimination of our husbands and it is up to us to reap revenge."

Greta told the ladies that her nephew was still living in the family home and she would speak to him and obtain information on the private air travel.

"I may be wrong but I was told they will be flying into Le Touquet in France, I will find out."

*

One of the ladies suggested that the method of dealing with Peter Horn and Nathan Garland should be discussed with Klaus.

"He has such valuable knowledge on espionage and how it works". Helga looked at Bertha.

"You are right; we could do with some help and advice."

Helga went to Klaus's office and she was immediately shown into his personal office.

She explained what had been discussed with the ladies and asked if he had any suggestions.

"Helga. I have just the man to help you and your ladies. His name is Viktor, no surname, just Viktor."

He asked his secretary to phone round to locate Viktor and tell him to report to my office.

His secretary took Helga into another small room and gave her a glass of wine.

"I will tell you when we can expect Viktor."

She left the room, closing the door behind her.

Ten minutes later the door opened and in walked Klaus accompanied by a tall dark haired young man.

Klaus introduced them and left the room.

"Now Helga, tell me what you have and what you want to achieve, do want them injured or eliminated?"

"They eliminated our husbands."

"If the two gentlemen are flying to the south of France, which, airport or airfield will they be flying from?"

"The last time they flew, it was from London City Airport."

"Good, give me your phone number and I will ring you when I have any news for you. Do they fly alone or do they take their bodyguards with them?"

"I am not too sure but the last time they flew to a meeting they flew by themselves."

*

Jan telephoned Peter and Nathan asking them to attend a meeting in the hotel in Paris in ten days time.

They both agreed to fly to France and motor to Paris. They could board a plane at the London City Airport and fly to Le Touque and stay in the Westminster Hotel overnight.

The following morning they planned to hire a car and motor to the hotel where the meeting is to be held in Paris. The journey will take 21/2 hours as it is 239Km, I understand it is a pleasant journey, mainly on the A16, Nathan looked at Peter.

"Are you happy with this arrangement?"

"Yes. Nathan I am."

The following morning, with the plans finalized, their official car called to collect them and take them to the City Airport on the day before the meeting.

Arriving at the airport, they were taken to a four-seater Cessna plane standing on the private runway. The pilot introduced himself to them and they boarded the plane. When seated, they fastened the seat belts, the pilot started up the engine and allowed it to run a while to warm up, the pilot was given permission to take off.

The City of London gradually faded behind them and the pilot steered the plane towards France, the English coast line came into view then gradually faded in the distance, the plane was flying very high as the air controllers had instructed.

Half way across the channel the engine started miss firing, the pilot looked at the fuel indicator and it registered a full tank, the engine spluttered and stopped.

The pilot turned to his passengers.

"Don't worry; I can glide quite a distance."

Suddenly he shouted.

"Good god, the ailerons are seized and I cannot control the tail plane or the flaps" and he lost control of the aircraft.

The propellers stopped turning and the plane nose dived, just before the aircraft hit the water, the plane exploded. The parts of the plane and its occupants was scattered on the surface of the sea.

The coast guard went out in response to their Mayday signal but they found very little floating on the surface of the sea. They spent two days searching but they drew a blank.

*

The Newspapers Headlines were full of the loss of two English M.P's, in the aircraft disaster. The coast guard scoured the sea in the area where the plane crashed but did not find any part of the plane which would indicate why the plane had crashed.

The only way to identify the occupants was due to the fact that the plane had been hired by a government department, of which, Nathan controlled.

The body parts were never found, the marine life would have disposed of them.

Viktor met up with Helga and Bella a week later. Helga looked at Viktor.

"How did you manage it?"

"A young man who works at the airfield and is sympathetic to our cause, he helped.

He fixed the fuel gauge to read full but it was not, the airilons were adjusted to seize after take off and maintain height. The explosion was engineered by using a pressure clock, which triggered off the explosion by the wind pressure caused by the aircraft plunging down from an extreme height. The explosion took place fifteen feet from the surface of the sea.

My name Viktor, is my professional name, it will never be used again as I am going back to a normal life.

I have a green grocery business in a small village near Hanover; it is being run by my wife and daughter while I am away."

He raised his right arm, saying.

"Heil Hitler."

Chapter 21

Bella and Helga visited Klaus.

"Hello. Ladies, I see you got you got two for the price of one."

"Yes Viktor did a good job." Klaus looked at them.

"One man who must not be injured or killed is Isaac Miller.

He did not kill Bill Funk; he was killed by a young Frenchman in revenge for Bill killing 15 villagers including the boy's mother and his two sisters some years ago during the war. If anything should happen to Miller I will be held responsible and charged by the police.

The man who was responsible for the death Pierre Ingles is Francoise Flowers. I am not sure where he is living now.

He must be living in France because he is or was employed by the French Government and he did live in Paris."

Looking at the two ladies, he said.

"Why did 75% of the families of the Nazi Officers marriages break up? Was it because of the unpleasant duties they were forced to perform and they took their work home with them and they became too unpleasant to live with, it is very sad Helga."

"However, I will organize my team to trace the whereabouts of Francoise Flowers, I am not too sure but I think his marriage has broken up. I will keep in touch but it might take a while to pin point Francoise's address."

"Klaus, the main reason for the family breakdown, is because when the men become officers they got inflated egos. The husbands were no longer the loving caring partners they once were; even their lovemaking became so brutal, verging on the brink of rape. The wives decided not to tolerate such behaviour any longer, the husbands were given the choice to leave the house or the wives and family would do so. There you have the real reason."

Klaus smiled, he got out of his chair and opened the door for the ladies to leave.

*

Helga telephoned Greta telling her that they were going after Francoise Flowers. He is the man the authorities are convinced he was the one who fed Pierre with a drug, which brought on a severe heart attack, which, killed him, although this was not the coroner's findings.

Greta said she could be relied upon to take part in the team to trace Francoise and reap her revenge for the killing of her husband. We will have to call a meeting to work out a plan of action and so a date for such a meeting was decided on.

Helga sat pondering and suddenly she looked up at Bella.

"How could we get Francoise into his car, close the garage door and attaché a pipe from the exhaust into the car to suffocate Francoise?"

"It is an option but how could we make him stay in the car, it is obvious he will attempt to get out of the car unless we find a way to force him to remain inside the car with the doors locked from the inside?"

"The plan is good, when we have all our ladies together at the meeting in two days time, we will put forward this plan asking for suggestions how it could be carried out.

One of the ladies may come up with a better plan which we can discuss."

Prior to the meeting Helga went to get advice from Klaus.

When she discussed her plan to him, he thought it ingenious but would need very careful planning.

"The ladies are meeting tomorrow to discuss options; I will come back to your office before we go ahead."

Helga smiled and left Klaus's office.

The three main committee members, Bella, Greta and Helga were the first to arrive at the hotel to ensure the reserved room was available.

They were very surprised when fifteen ladies arrived. The ladies who had lost their husbands had brought either a family member or friends. The widows were taken to another room asked if they would vouch for the ladies they had brought with them. There must be no slip up due to their inclusion at the meeting by a mole.

"The 18 ladies sat round in a circle, Helga stood up and welcomed them all. She then proceeded to outline the plan they were considering but unable to complete. If any one of you can suggest how to complete the jig saw please speak up. Has any one got an alternative plan? Enjoy the drinks laid out on the table and enjoy talking to each other and perhaps you will come up with a plan?"

The ladies sat around talking, suddenly Heidi jumped up.

"Could we force drink on him until he is virtually unconscious then start the engine, lock the car doors and bring down the up and over garage door and attaché a pipe from the exhaust and feed the pipe through the rear seats to inside the car."

"Brilliant, we must fine tune how we can force the drink down him and attend to the engine, should he come to and attempt to switch off the engine.

The car doors will have to be locked from the outside; giving the impression he has locked from the inside. We will have to get copies of Francoise car keys.

"When my husband lost his original set of car keys, he had to supply the engine and chassis numbers to get a replacement set of keys."

"Right, we must firstly obtain a set of keys for Francoise's car or copies and the monitor to open and close his automatic garage up and over door."

"Ladies this is our first step."

Klaus telephoned Helga,"

Enquiring if they had made any progress with their plans?"

Helga told him briefly of their plan.

"Bring all the ladies to my office tomorrow afternoon and I will arrange that the large room is vacant."

*

Helga and the thirteen ladies went along to Klaus's office and they shown into the large room, who, should be in the room but Frank Kessler and Fritz Beckenbaugh.

They were greeted , when the ladies removed their coats, they were all wearing a Blouse in light fawn and a Dark brown skirt as they wore as Ladies Nazi uniform a few years back. When they took their arms from the coats they displayed the Nazi Armbands. Kessler and Beckenbaugh loudly applauded them.

Klaus quickly went into his office and retrieved his armband from his desk draw and quickly slipped it on his left arm. When Kessler and Beckenbaugh removed their coats, they too were wearing the armbands, they raised their right arms shouting Heil Hitler and Klaus and the ladies responded.

Kessler said.

"Please be seated."

"I am so proud to see you all wearing the uniform of the ladies movement. I am still confident that the dream of our wonderful Fuhrer to dominate Europe will come about; we failed using force, now we will achieve his objective by crafty political maneuvering. Our object is achievable but it may take a year or so but it will happen.

I understand you wish to eliminate Francoise Flowers.

The copies of his car keys and the garage monitor will be available tomorrow and will be delivered to this office.

Now I will pass you over to Fritz Beckenbaugh, most of you will know Fritz was one of the most decorated officers of the Third Reich."

.He stood up and received a thunderous applause, as the applause died down, he said.

"Thank you ladies; I have given a lot of thought to your plan to eliminate Francoise Flowers. You are right; it will be the better plan to deal with him in his own garage and made to appear as he has taken his own life.

Frank has told you that the car keys and monitor will be available tomorrow but leave it a few days to enable us to get a complete picture of his activities. We will make a man available to restrain Francoise, while the vodka or whisky, or whatever spirit you decide to use is poured down his throat. Shall we arrange the date through Klaus? The plan will be laid out but it is up to you ladies, the date of your choice."

*

Klaus felt more confident about his position now he had involved Kessler and Beckenbaugh in the espionage. Klaus smiled to himself, they like to think they are in charge but they are not, the ladies are. Several days later, Klaus received a telephone call from Kessler telling him that Francoise's family is going away for a few days holiday.

"While his family is away, he will visit the same restaurant each evening and he arrives home at 7.30.

I will send Heinrich to wait inside the garage using the copy monitor, perhaps one of the ladies, or perhaps two could wait in the garage with him. Heinrich can restrain him while the ladies use a funnel to pour the alcohol into his mouth. Gerta will want to take part?"

Right, tomorrow night it is?"

Heinrich and three of the ladies waited in a car away from Francoise's house waiting for the darkness to close in.

They got out of the car and approached the house, they made sure no neighbours were about and raised the garage door sufficiently enough to enable them to get in.

Waiting seemed an eternity but suddenly they heard a car approaching and the garage door started to rise.

Heinrich had hidden himself on the left hand side among a load of garden tools and other rubbish. The car came into the garage and the door was closing behind him.

Francoise switched off the engine and as he opened the car door, Heinrich gripped him by his shoulders and forced him back on to the car seat. Helga pinched his nose and as he opened his mouth Greta pushed the funnel into his mouth and poured whisky into his mouth from the bottle .He was spluttering and trying to resist but with four people dealing with him, he couldn't move.

The bottle of whisky was almost empty; Helga passed the second bottle to Greta who was enjoying her revenge. They had taken precautions by wearing latex rubber gloves. Françoise stopped resisting as Greta poured the second bottle into the funnel which was going direct into his stomach.

Helga started the car engine and Bella attached a pipe on to the exhaust pipe passing it through the rear seats inside the car.

Greta put one of the bottles in Francoise hand and Heinrich put on a small gas mask, Helga, Greta and Bella operated the garage door and they went outside, using a copy monitor to lower the garage door behind them.

Heinrich checked to ensure Francoise was breathing in the exhaust fumes, when his breathing became much lower, he locked the car doors and raised the door to leave the garage.

When the door was lowered it was still possible to see the fumes escaping under the door.

They walked back down the road to their car, and left the area.

"Ladies, all went well; I hope the result is satisfactory."

Several days later the newspaper was full of the story that Francoise Flowers a most influential minister of the French Government had committed suicide while his family was away on holiday.

The inquest was carried out and the coroner carried out an in depth enquiry into the minister's death. His verdict was that Francoise had taken his own life, for what reasons, we shall never know. Helga visited Klaus, he was all smiles.

"Wonderful job Helga, terrifying how easy you have carried out this task."

Chapter 22

Several months later Heidi contacted Helga.

"I have been investigating, or should I say I have been bribing and the name I have come up with is Boris Bormann. He was the man responsible for my Robin's death."

"Right Heidi, I will contact Klaus and enquire if he has heard any rumours about Robins death?"

Helga telephoned Klaus and he invited her to his office the same day.

As she entered his office, he stood up to greet her and offered her a chair, his secretary brought her a glass of dry white wine, for which, she remembered Helga asked for on her last visit. Helga then told him that Heidi had contacted her saying that it was Boris Bormann responsible for her Robin's death.

"I have heard that name mentioned before Helga. Give me a few days and I will ask my undercover agents to sniff around. Ring me in three days time."

Helga telephoned Heidi, telling her that Klaus was looking into her claim and that she was to ring in a few days time."

Helga put the phone down, she sat day dreaming.

Why did Robin feel it necessary to keep chasing other women when Heidi was a tall blonde haired lady with a wonderful figure and a very attractive woman although she was approaching middle age? But so was he.

It was common knowledge that Robin was a womanizer and Heidi must have had her own suspicions.

The way he attended a gym several times each week to stave off the threat of a thickening waist line and his dress was always meticulous.

*

Boris and his wife enjoy spending their holidays with their married children and grandchildren and it was planned they would join them for one week. Both of their sons-in-law enjoy joining Boris with his favourite pastime, which is mountain climbing, his wife, on many occasion tried to persuade him to give up such a dangerous hobby but he flatly refused to do so.

This year Boris decided to rent a chalet just on the outskirts of Courmayeur in the Oasta Valley, it is quite large and it will sleep eight people and there are several folding beds suitable for children, it will be very comfortable and not over crowded.

The families were all looking forward to sharing the holiday, it was arranged to meet up at the chalet and each family was travelling from different parts of Germany.

Boris was really excited; he had never attempted to climb such a high mountain. Mount Blanc rises to 15,782 feet above sea level. It is sometimes referred to as "La Dame Blanche" which you, as my readers will know it is French for "The White Lady" and he regarded it as a challenge.

Boris and Paula arrived at the chalet first and Paula fussed around making sure the bedding etc was okay, while she was doing this Boris dealt with lighting a log fire, when he got the flames reflecting on the walls and furniture inside the chalet, it looked really inviting.

Later that day one of their son's and his family arrived; he smiled at Boris, when he opened the car boot to remove the suitcases, his climbing gear was on view and Boris looked at him and winked.

They decided not to eat until the other family had arrived. When the other family did arrive, they all went down to the village hotel for dinner; it was a most enjoyable evening.

The grandchildren were excited; they were hoping they would be able to go on the novices ski slope. Both mothers are expert skiers so they should be in safe hands.

*

Helga was surprised to receive a phone call from Klaus.

"My agent has been checking around and he is 99.9% sure that Boris was responsible for the death of Robin Grenfell, at least he instigated it. Boris and his family are at present staying in a chalet on the outskirts of Courmayer in the Oasta Valley and he will be attempting to climb various parts of Mount Blanc.

This might give you an opportunity to deal with him; he has rented the chalet for one month. You must ask your ladies to come up with plans how to arrange a tragic accident.

When they have formulated any plans may I suggest you hold a meeting to decide on the most practical plan put forward, do you agree?"

"Yes, I will call our ladies together, explain where Boris is staying and his hobby of climbing and arrange a meeting three days later."

"That sounds right to me Helga, keep me informed."

When the ladies meeting was convened, Klaus had asked to be present.

Helga stood up saying,

"Have any lady come up with a plan?"

Three of the ladies stood up, Helga laughed.

"My word, you have been busy."

"Right Bella, what is your plan?"

"Fashion a dagger in ice and insert it up his nostril or in the ear into the brain, the ice would melt leaving no evidence of the dagger." Klaus looked up.

"Good thinking but the flesh tissues will have been torn and it will look deliberate but we must think about it."

Giselle stood up.

"When he is climbing, could we arrange an avalanche to overcome him and be suffocated."

"Yes that is another good suggestion."

They were all surprised when Bertha stood up.

"As you are all aware, I am still engaged as a doctor, my idea would be to inject an air bubble into the bloodstream using a hypodermic needle. Death would be almost instantaneous and the coroner would sum up the death as due to a severe stroke."

"I must congratulate you ladies on your ideas but you will have discuss how one of them could be carried out and make it look like an accident. In each case it will be necessary to have close contact, which could be difficult."

As Klaus looked around the room, his staring eyes made several of the ladies feel uncomfortable.

"The ideal situation would be if he is caught up in an avalanche and in need of medical attention that would be when Bertha comes into the picture.

A lot of ifs and buts' but it could be made to happen and ladies we will make it happen."

*

The following day Boris and one of his sons–in-law went climbing on one part of Mount Blanc; they chose to walk up gentle slope to view the various sheer faces of ice. This suited one of the boys as he is unable to climb due to a broken collar bone when he was involved in a car accident two weeks earlier.

They all enjoyed the walk and they later called at a bar for a drink before going back to the chalet. As they sat down enjoying their drink, they decided that they would try a small rock face the following day.

Klaus telephoned Helga, saying that a small chalet overlooking Boris's chalet has been made available for the ladies and transport will be made available

Helga contacted Bertha and Giselle inviting them to join her in the chalet.

Boris and his wife spent a most enjoyable week with their family but his daughter would not allow her husband to go on any dangerous climbs. She implored her father not to endanger her husband as they have two young children and another on the way, she did not consider it fair that he should take any chances. Boris totally agreed with her.

He decided to leave the sheer faces to until he is climbing by himself over the next three weeks.

The families had gone home and Boris and Paula visited the surrounding villages which they both enjoyed but Boris was anxious to try climbing a vertical sheer ice face which he regards as a challenge.

*

This particular morning Boris assembled his climbing gear ready for the off but Paula insisted that they had breakfast and he helped her change the bedding for her to put in the washer.

The weather forecast was not good and the main concern was with the very strong winds, in fact, it was referred to as a weather warning.

In spite of Paula's argument and concern, Boris set off to go climbing.

He arrived at the face he was going to attempt to climb; he put his crampons on over his boots and the pitons and a hammer in his waist belt.

He climbed about fifteen feet from the ground when a very strong gust of wind made him cling to the pitons but he kept climbing to about forty feet up, again he had to hang on to the pitons driven into the ice and the rope he tied to them. He was just about to give up and climb down when a terrific gust of wind caught him and he fell.

When he hit the ground on his back, he lost consciousness and when he came round he could not move, he realized that he must have injured himself badly. As he laid there he became covered with snow, the strong winds had created an avalanche. The first aid men going around found him covered in snow and they strapped him on flat board and put him on an ambulance.

The local radio station interrupted its program, announcing the due to the freak weather conditions, strong winds has caused an avalanche which has injured a lot of climbers and in view of the numbers, any person with medical knowledge should report to the local hospital to help.

Bertha immediately went to the hospital, she felt that her medical expertise would be a great help.

As the casualties were wheeled in, the doctors divided the nurses into teams, some to attend to cuts and bruises and the more experienced nurses to deal with fractures and broken bones. One of the senior doctors regonised Bertha.

"Bertha, we have one patient coming in who fell on his back and is unable to move, I want you to take charge of him, and I know you are very experienced in this field. Here he comes, he was being wheeled in on a stretcher, leave him with Doctor Spiers she will decide on his treatment."

"What is his name?"

"Boris Bormann."

They wheeled him into a cubicle and a young man helped Bertha to remove his clothing to enable them to investigate his injuries. The young man looked at Bertha.

"He looks like a goner to me."

Bertha thought to herself, "He soon will be."

"Get me a bag of saline and I will attaché a drip in an attempt to overcome shock."

She located a vein in the back of his hand and inserted a cannula to make it ready for the needle to be inserted but before he came back with the bag she inserted the air bubble and when he came back, Bertha attached the saline drip to the patient's hand.

"He is fairly comfortable; we must go and deal with any one else needing help"

Eventually, all the casualties' who had been brought into the hospital had received initial attention, now it was time to go back and investigate their injuries in depth.

The rescue teams had been alerted and gone into the mountains to search for any injured climbers unable to help themselves.

The matron checked on the injured and found that five climbers have not survived in spite of the medical expertise; one of the dead was Boris. Several of the deaths were caused by suffocation being buried in the snow when they were caught up in the avalanche. Of the injured three were critical but the remaining eight appear to be progressing well.

The x-ray department will be busy for many hours.

Chapter 23

Klaus had been made aware of Isaac being followed and obviously being targeted and in view of the police telling him he will be responsible should Isaac come to any harm he decided to visit the police headquarters.

He made an appointment to visit the police commissioner and told him of the fact that Isaac is being followed and he is in no way responsible.

"Officer Gunter, I believe you, someone is trailing Isaac Miller, we have no reason to suspect you and so far we are unable to understand why, or by whom. You have no need to worry; we realize that it is nothing to do with you. In fact, when we do trace the person or persons responsible we contact you.

*

The avenging widows met up at Helga's house to discuss a message confirming that Isaac was responsible for the death of Bill Funk and Herman Brant. Our next target is Isaac Miller; we shall need a complete dossier on his daily habits.

"I think our activity will have to centre on his warehouse. It is a small warehouse and he employs three ladies to work just Thursday and Friday of each week. Their duties are to attend to incoming goods, label and place on the designated shelving racks to make the goods easily identifiable.

When the incoming goods have been dealt with, they then wrap and address goods to be dispatched.

Those two days are the only time that there is any activity in the warehouse; Isaac is in the warehouse every day of the week to attend to reordering and to attend to incoming telephone orders or enquiries, No, Monday he visits his customers and his suppliers."

Helga and the other avenging ladies gave a lot of thought to how to deal with Isaac.

Bella being the widow of Bill Funk insisted that she should be advised of any plans that one of the ladies might come up with, they discussed many ideas but not one appeared to be a satisfactory answer.

They discussed shooting, poisoning, suffocation and other ways to end Isaac's life. Helga turned to Bella.

"You were trained as an explosive expert, surely you can think of some way?"

"Yes I have, my first thought was to create an explosion when he flushed the toilet in his office." All the ladies looked at Bella.

"What's wrong with that idea?"

"I will tell you, the warehouse is securely locked and the entire interior is covered by infra red security system."

"Why not speak to Klaus, I feel sure he will know a man or women capable to shut down the system, long enough to enable the booby trap to be set?"

When Helga spoke to Klaus, he told her of his visit to the police headquarters to ensure he would not be held responsible for Isaac's injuries or death. They are aware Isaac is being tailed and they no longer suspect me.

"Klaus. If you wanted to visit a small warehouse, that had the interior covered by infra-red security in every nook and cranny, who would you speak to for advice of how-to close it down for about twenty minutes?"

"I know several such people but the best is expensive."

"Recommend one and I will approach him."

"The one I am thinking of is female."

"Better still, she will speak a female's language.

*

Helga was at home when the door bell rang, she went to the door and a tall beautiful slim, blonde haired lady stood on the door step.

"Are you Helga?"

"Yes, who are you?"

"My name is Hemuet, Klaus asked me to visit and he thought you might wish to speak with me?"

"Do come in Hemuet."

"Helga, Klaus briefed me what you wanted of me. I feel sure we can work something out together."

"Would it be convenient to you if I called the ladies together tomorrow night and then we thrash out the details?"

"Certainly, I have asked Klaus to obtain a complete diagram showing where the security control box is situated and the position of the toilet in relation to the entry door."

"Oh! Also, he says he can arrange to get a key made. Tomorrow evening I will be here to meet your ladies or should I say "The revenging widows." "That is how Klaus refers to your ladies."

The following evening, they all met up up at Helga's house and Bella explained what she had in mind.

"Will you ask him to check the toilet; is it flushed using a handle or a plunger on top of the system?"

I need to know because the trigger will need to be set differently."

They sat round chatting for the next hour, when Hemuet left she promised she would be in contact when she has the key and the diagram.

*

The following evening Hemuet decided to walk along to Isaac's warehouse, looking round to ensure no one was about, she pushed the probe through the letter box and pressed the button hoping it would deactivate the security system but it had the complete reverse effect, the alarm bells began ringing loudly. Hemeut removed the probe and walked away.

She contacted Klaus, asking if he knew the make of the security system control box as her probe would need the frequency recalibrating to close down the alarm system.

Two days later Helga received the diagram indicating the position of the toilet in the private office and advising it was operated with a handle to flush also the make and type of the security system box, which controls the warehouse's safety net.

Hemeut telephoned Helga telling her that the probe used failed, but she was delighted when Helga told her the type and make of the security box.

"Thank you, I will work on the system and try again before Bella is ready to create her little surprise for Isaac."

Hemeut, expertly adjusted the wavelength on the probe and decided to try it out again that evening.

She strolled along the pavement to Isaac's warehouse; she said loudly, "Here goes."

She pushed the probe through the letter box and pressed the button and there was a click, indicating the turn off switch had been activated and the alarm did not ring out this time. Hemeut held her breath as she pressed the button again to switch the system on again, Hemeut was delighted.

Helga called her team of "Avenging Widows" to a meeting to be held in her house.

"Good evening ladies." As Helga welcomed the ladies, Hemeut walked in.

"Our friend here has managed to come up with an instrument that will shut down Isaac's safety net and I have two keys for the main door. Now we will have to decide what day shall we put our plan into operation?" Giselle said,

"This one is causing a lot of trouble, why not just shoot him and be done with it?"

They all started laughing.

"Right ladies, when?" Bella said,

"I will go in on Sunday night if Hemeut is agreeable?"

"Sunday night is okay with me Bella; I am getting well paid for this job, so any night you wish.

We will agree on a time when the meeting is closed."

They met after the meeting and arranged to meet at 1am Monday morning.

Sunday evening Bella was very apprehensive about the whole plan but she was determined to go ahead with the plan, this man killed my husband and her children's father.

She put on a heavy coat, collected her explosive material and a flashlight and then set off to meet Hemeut.

They met at the warehouse and Hemeut inserted the probe through the letter box and pressed the button, they heard the click as the system shut down.

*

Bella inserted the key very carefully and turning the key slowly with a trembling hand, she held her breath as she pushed the door open; they both breathed a sigh of relief when the alarm did not start to ring.

Bella went into the building using her torchlight, she located the office door, and she went in and saw the door leading to the private toilet

She removed the top cover of the toilet and she attached the trigger to the flushing arm, this should activate the explosive. Replaced the top cover, she closed the office door and locked the main door.

Hemeut again put the probe through the letter box; they heard a click as the security system was reactivated. They hugged each other.

"Job done."

Bella telephoned Helga telling her that they have had a most enjoyable evening and they look forward to the next music session.

"Good, I am so pleased you enjoyed the evening."

Monday morning Isaac left home at his usual time and went into his office. He threw his brief case on to the desktop and plugged in the kettle in the wall plug. It came to the boil and he made himself a cup of coffee and then went through all the papers on his desk. Having cleared his desk, he sat back to enjoy his coffee. He decided to visit one of his customers but he would have to tidy himself up in the bathroom, he threw the tissues he used to dry his hands in the toilet and he flushed it.

There was a terrific explosion and the surrounding area was completely devastated. When the police and the ambulance arrived it was obvious it was going to be difficult to put the correct body parts in his coffin.

The explosion was announced on the radio and in the evening the devastation was shown on Television.

Bernie was terribly upset to think he had failed to protect Isaac.

*

The coroner carried out a thorough investigation into the inquest of Isaac's death. Several of the Gas Board Executives were called to the stand, it was thought a ruptured gas pipe had leaked and a cigarette packet and a lighter had been found among the rubble. Had there been a build up of gas from the leaking pipe, in the enclosed space of the toilet compartment, which was ignited when Herr Miller lit a cigarette?

In spite of an in depth investigation no definite answer could be found for the explosion, no explosive material could be found.

When the coroner summed it all up, he decided to leave it as an open verdict. There is no proof that any one person can be held responsible.

Bella attended the inquest and she smiled when the coroner gave his verdict.

"You can now rest in peace Bill."

It is obvious she was not aware of the atrocities he was responsible for in the past, which contributed to his death.

Several days later the ladies met at Helga's house, as each lady arrived and removed their coats, every one was wearing a brown shirt.

They sat chatting and Hemeut walked in and they were all very surprised, she too was wearing a brown shirt.

Helga stood up and told them that Isaac had met his death, they all raised their glasses.

"The toast is to our dead husbands. We have avenged their deaths, what next?"

CHAPTER 24

The British Intelligence team summoned Ken Lee, Major Lance Goodchild and Jon von Krupp to a meeting in London urgently. When they arrived at Admiralty House, they were directed to a room, which was furnished like a board room of a large public company with a long highly polished table with one chair at the head and chairs down each side. They were served with a drink of their choice and the Prime Minister and three of his ministers walked into the room.

"Gentlemen, thank you for coming at such short notice but we have recently made a disturbing discovery.

Nathan and Peter were not killed in an aircraft accident as originally thought but they were murdered.

Parts of the aircraft have recently been washed up on the beaches of Jersey.

On inspection, it was discovered that the ailerons had been sabotaged, when the engine failed, the plane could not be controlled by using the flaps to glide and being a light aircraft, this should have been possible. The second item, the explosion, this was triggered by an air pressure tube gauging the pressure caused by its rapid descent." Lance glanced at Ken.

"This has the finger prints of Klaus Gunter all over it."

"This name has come up several times lately and in view of this we investigated and we found that he is was a senior army officer in the Nazi movement but for some reason he didn't stand trial in Nuremberg. What shall we do about this man?" The PM sat down with a smile on his face.

"Leave him to us sir"

"I will but if anything should go wrong, I will deny knowing any of you. We can't have the government embarrassed in any way as we are engaged in several sensitive international meetings."

The PM and his ministers got out of their chairs and left the room after shaking hands.

Jan left when the meeting was closed as he had another meeting to attend. Ken and Lance decided to have lunch before going home. Lance felt too tired to go back to his office.

*

Arriving home, Lance's wife Pat, could see he was tired out. He got undressed and stepped into the shower, when he was showered he changed into his old clothes, in which, he felt relaxed. While he had been showering, Pat had placed a tray with tea and cakes next to his favourite chair in the conservatory.

The fact that Nathan and Peter had been targeted and killed had unnerved him. He had considered signing on for another few years beyond his retirement date but this had changed his mind. He would help Ken Lee with the Klaus project but after that he would retire. He wouldn't tell Ken of his decision, otherwise he would do his utmost to persuade him to stay on.

It was a beautiful sunny afternoon with a few clouds in the sky, in those clouds he could see the faces of his friends he lost during the war but he did not expect to lose Peter in peacetime, he felt so depressed.

Yes, enough is enough.

Several days later Jon telephoned Ken and Lance telling them that Klaus has completely disappeared off the screen, no one has seen or heard of him for quite a while.

"I had left a message at Bernie's office asking him to ring me."

Bernie received Jon's message and he was quite intrigued.

Jon's phone rang, when he picked up the receiver, the man on the other end of the line said.

"Returning your call, shall we meet?"

Jan realized who it was immediately.

"Yes, is tomorrow morning at ten o'clock at you favourite coffee bar, will that be convenient?"

"Yes, that will be fine?"

Bernie arrived first; he had a pot of coffee and two cognacs' on the table when Jan arrived a few minutes later.

"Now Jan, what is your problem?"

"I was instructed to have Klaus Gunter followed and submit a full dossier on his daily movements but my teams cannot find him and they are blanked out when they ask questions regarding his whereabouts."

"Let us enjoy our coffee and cognacs and I will arrange for your enquiries to be investigated by my team, they could do with some work."

They spent a pleasant half an hour talking about their families and their future. Jon was surprised when Bernie told him that his son had gone into politics and now held a position in the Israeli government.

"Good luck to him Bernie, there is a lot of work to be done sorting out the world today, those with a little want a lot but those with a lot are very reluctant to let go."

"That is very well said Jan, however, I will put your enquiries in motion when I get back to my office, I will ring you even it is only a sniff they can find out about Klaus."

"Jan spoke to Ken Lee telling him that Klaus had disappeared but Bernie has put his team to work trying to trace him. He doesn't hold much hopes of locating him, they have checked the obituary records and the hospitals, you name it they have tried every avenue."

*

Several days later Bernie rang Ken saying he had just received news of Klaus's location.

"He is in a nursing home in the suburbs of Berlin; in English it is called The Green Pastures. I cannot tell you anymore at this stage but I will visit the nursing home tomorrow and will ring you later."

The following morning, Bernie confirmed the exact location of the nursing home before leaving his office.

Arriving at the nursing home, he rang the door bell, a nurse opened the door.

"Good morning sir, how can I help you?"

"Have you a patient named Klaus Gunter?"

"Yes, are you family?"

" A very close friend."

"I will ask the matron if you will be allowed to visit him."

The matron came out of her office.

"You say you are a close friend, when did you last speak to him?"

"It must be two or three months ago."

"Right, when you go into his room, please, don't allow your face to reflect your dismay when you look at him?"

Bernie entered Klaus's room, he was appalled at Klaus's condition, he was just skin and bone, it was Klaus. Bernie was really taken aback.

Klaus opened his eyes and looked up. Seeing Bernie, he tried to smile.

"Have you come to gloat?" he spoke with great difficulty.

"I have not come to gloat, I am extremely sorry to see you in such a situation, is there anything I can do to help you?"

"Thanks but no."

"I am told that I have terminal cancer and my family is coming tomorrow, the doctor has given me three more days to remain among the living. I would have preferred to have been shot while protecting my fatherland than suffering like I am now.

I am now having nightmares, I hear the screams of men trapped in an English tank during the battles in Tobruk, three of our tanks encircled the tank and used their flamethrowers, the tank glowed and the occupants were killed by the heat. My one regret Bernie, prior to my illness I did not believe one could get so much comfort from prayer."

Bernie sat by Klaus's bedside, unsure what to say or do. While he sat pondering, Klaus went to sleep.

Bernie stood up and quietly walked out of the room.

He went to the matron's office to thank her for allowing him to visit.

"It is sad for a human being to end their days in such a manner."

That evening Bernie telephoned Ken and Jon explaining his visit to the nursing home and Klaus's terminal illness and in each case they expressed regret that he should end his days in such a manner.

THE END

Other books by Ron Walters:

Our Dan	ISBN: 978 1 84549 239 7
Our Dan's 5th Column	ISBN: 978 1 84549 403 2
The Younger Son	ISBN: 978 1 84549 385 1

(All published by arima Publishing)